THE MARAKAIOS BABY

BY

KATE HEWITT

This is a work of fiction. Names, characters, places, locations and incidents are purely fictional and bear no relationship to any real life individuals, living or dead, or to any actual places, business establishments, locations, events or incidents. Any resemblance is entirely coincidental.

Published in Great Britain 2015
by Mills & Boon, an imprint of Harlequin (UK) Limited,
Eton House, 18-24 Paradise Road, Richmond, Surrey, TW9 1SR

ISBN: 978-0-263-24901-9

Harlequin (UK) Limited's policy is to use papers that are natural, renewable and recyclable products and made from wood grown in sustainable forests. The logging and manufacturing processes conform to the legal environmental regulations of the country of origin.

Printed and bound in Spain

After spending three years as a die-hard New Yorker, **Kate Hewitt** now lives in a small village in the English Lake District with her husband, their five children and a golden retriever. In addition to writing intensely emotional stories she loves reading, baking, and playing chess with her son—she has yet to win against him, but she continues to try.

Learn more about Kate at www.kate-hewitt.com

Books by Kate Hewitt

Mills & Boon® Modern™ Romance

Kholodov's Last Mistress
The Undoing of de Luca

The Marakaios Brides

The Marakaios Marriage

The Chatsfield

Virgin's Sweet Rebellion

Rivals to the Crown of Kadar

Captured by the Sheikh
Commanded by the Sheikh

The Diomedi Heirs

The Prince She Never Knew
A Queen for the Taking?

The Bryants: Powerful & Proud

Beneath the Veil of Paradise
In the Heat of the Spotlight
His Brand of Passion

The Power of Redemption

The Darkest of Secrets
The Husband She Never Knew

Visit the author profile page at millsandboon.co.uk for more titles

To Lauren,
Thank you for your many years of friendship. Love, K.

CHAPTER ONE

'WILL YOU MARRY ME?'

The question seemed to bounce off the walls and echo through the room as Marguerite Ferrars stared in shock at the face of the man who had asked the question—her lover, Leonidas Marakaios.

He gazed at her with a faint half-smile quirking his lips, his eyebrows slightly raised. In his hand he held a small black velvet box, and the solitaire diamond of who knew how many carats inside sparkled with quiet sophistication.

'Margo?'

His voice was lilting, teasing; he thought she was silent because she was so surprised. But, while that was true, she felt something else as well. Appalled. *Terrified.*

She'd never expected this—never thought that charismatic playboy Leo would think of *marriage.* A lifetime commitment, a life—and love—you could lose. And she knew the searing pain of losing someone—the way it left you breathless and gasping, waking up in the night, your face awash in tears, even years later…

The moment stretched on too long, and still she said nothing. She couldn't. Because she didn't dare say yes and yet no seemed just as impossible. Leo Marakaios was not a man who accepted refusal. Rejection.

She watched as a slight frown pulled his eyebrows together and he withdrew the hand holding the open velvet box to rest it in his lap.

'Leo…' she began finally, helplessly—because how could she tell this impossibly arrogant, handsome, charismatic man no? And yet she had to. Of course she had to.

'I didn't think this would be *that* much of a surprise,' he said, his voice holding only a remnant of lightness now.

She felt a surge of something close to anger, which was almost a relief. 'Didn't you? We've never had the kind of relationship that…'

'That what?' He arched an eyebrow, the gesture caught between wryness and disdain.

She could feel him withdrawing, and while she knew she should be glad, she felt only a deep, wrenching sorrow. This wasn't what she'd wanted. But she didn't—couldn't—want marriage either. Couldn't let someone matter that much.

'That…led somewhere,' she finished, and he closed the box with a snap, his expression turning so terribly cold.

'I see.'

Words stuck in her throat—the answer she knew she had to give yet somehow couldn't make herself say. 'Leo, we've never even talked about the future.'

'We've been together for two years,' he returned. 'I think it's reasonable to assume it was *going somewhere*.'

His voice held a deliberate edge, and his eyes were blazing silver fire. Or maybe ice, for he looked so cold now—even contemptuous. And moments ago he'd been asking to marry her. It almost seemed laughable.

'Together for two years,' Margo allowed, determined to stay reasonable, 'but we've hardly had what most people would call a "normal" relationship. We've met in strange cities, in restaurants and hotels—'

'Which is how you wanted it.'

'And how you wanted it too. It was an *affair*, Leo. A—a fling.'

'A two-year fling.'

She rose from her chair, agitated now, and paced in front of the picture window that overlooked the Île de la Cité. It was so strange and unsettling to have Leo here in her apartment, her sanctuary, when he'd never come to her home before. Restaurants and hotels, yes—anonymous places for emotionless no-strings sex…that was what they'd *agreed*. That was all she could let herself have.

The risk of trying for more was simply too great. She knew what it was like to lose everything—even your own soul. She couldn't go through that again. She *wouldn't*.

Not even for Leo.

'You seem upset,' Leo remarked tonelessly.

'I just didn't expect this.'

'As it happens, neither did I.'

He rose from where he'd been sitting, on the damask settee she'd upholstered herself, his tall, rangy figure seeming to fill the cosy space of her sitting room. He looked wrong here, somehow, amidst all her things—her throw pillows and porcelain ornaments; he was too big, too dark, too powerful…like a tiger pacing the cage of a kitten.

'I thought most women wanted to get married,' he remarked.

She turned on him then, another surge of anger making her feel strong. 'What a ridiculous, sexist assumption! And I, in any case, am *not* "most women".'

'No,' Leo agreed silkily. 'You're not.'

His eyes blazed with intent then—an intent that made Margo's breath catch in her chest.

The sexual chemistry between them had been instantaneous—electric. She remembered catching sight of him in a hotel bar in Milan two years ago. She'd been nursing a single glass of white wine while she went over her notes for the next day's meeting. He'd strolled over to the bar and slid onto the stool next to hers, and the little hairs on the back of her neck had prickled. She'd felt as if she were finally coming alive.

She'd gone back with him to his room that night. It had been so unlike her—she'd always kept herself apart, her heart on ice. In her twenty-nine years she'd had only two lovers before Leo, both of them lamentably forgettable. Neither of those men had affected her the way Leo did—and not just physically.

From that first night he'd reached a place inside her she'd thought numb, dead. He'd brought her back to life. And while she'd known it was dangerous she'd stayed with him, because the thought of *not* being with Leo was worse.

Except now that was a reality. She'd thought an affair with Leo would be safe, that he would never ask more of her than she was prepared to give. But here he was asking for marriage, a lifetime, and her response was bone-deep terror.

Which was why she could not accept his proposal.

Except she had a terrible and yet thrilling certainty that he had a different proposal in mind now, as he came towards her, his gaze turning hooded and sleepy even though that lithe, powerful body she knew almost as well as her own was taut with suppressed energy and tension.

She licked her lips, felt the insistent thud of her heart, the stirring of blood in her veins. Even now her body yearned for him.

'Leo…'

'You surprise me, Margo.'

She gave a little shake of her head. 'You're the one who surprised *me*.'

'Clearly. But I thought you'd be pleased. Don't you want to get married?'

He sounded so reasonable, but she saw a certain calculation in his eyes, and he ran one hand up and down her bare arm, so gooseflesh broke out in the wake of his touch.

'No.'

'Why not?'

His easy, interested tone jarred with the fingers he continued to run up and down her arm, and with that sleepy, knowing gaze.

'I'm a career woman, Leo—'

'You can be a *married* career woman, Margo. This is the twenty-first century, after all.'

'Oh? And how would that work, exactly? You live in central Greece—the middle of nowhere. How am I supposed to work from there?'

For a second she thought she saw a gleam of something like triumph in his eyes, but then it sparked out and he gave a negligent shrug of his shoulders. 'You could commute. The flight from Athens to Paris is only a few hours.'

'Commute? Are you serious?'

'We could work something out, Margo, if that's all that's stopping you.'

There was a note of challenge in his voice, and she realised then what he was doing. Leonidas Marakaios was a powerful and persuasive man. He was CEO of the Marakaios Enterprises, a company that had started with a few olive groves and a cold press and was now a multibillion dollar company—a man of the world who was used to getting what he wanted. And he wanted her. So here he was, breaking down her defences, discarding her arguments. And the trouble was she was so weak, so tempted, that it might actually work.

She turned away from him to take a few steadying

breaths without him seeing how unsettled she was. In the darkness of the window she could see her reflection: a too pale face, wide eyes, and a tumble of long dark brown hair that fell nearly to her waist.

When Leo had shown up twenty minutes ago she'd been in yoga pants and a faded tee shirt, her face without a lick of make-up, her hair down. She'd been silently appalled. She'd always been careful that he saw only the woman she wanted him to—the woman the world saw: sexy, chic, professional, a little bit distant, a little bit cool. All their meetings had been stage-managed affairs; she'd swept into a restaurant or hotel room in full make-up, a sexy little negligee in her bag, insouciant and secure.

He'd never seen her like this: vulnerable, without the mask of make-up, the armour of designer clothes. He'd never seen her agitated and uncertain, her *savoir-faire* slipping from her fingers.

'Margo,' Leo said quietly. 'Tell me the real reason.'

Another quick breath, buoying inside her lungs. 'I told you, Leo. I don't want marriage or what it entails. The whole housewife routine bores me to death.' She made her voice cold—careless, even.

Steeling herself, she turned around to face him and nearly flinched at the careful consideration in his eyes. She had a horrible feeling she wasn't fooling him at all.

'I just said you don't need to be a housewife. Do you think I want to change you completely?'

'You don't even know me, Leo, not really.'

He took a step towards her, and again she saw that intent in his eyes, felt an answering flare inside her. She had, she realised, just given him a challenge.

'Are you sure about that?'

'I'm not talking about sex.'

'What don't I know, then?' He spread his hands wide, his eyebrows raised. 'Tell me.'

'It's not that simple.'

'Because you don't want it to be. I *know* you, Margo. I know your feet get cold in the middle of the night and you tuck them between my legs to keep them warm. I know you like marshmallows even though you pretend you don't eat any sweets.'

She almost laughed at that. 'How do you know about the marshmallows?' Her dirty little secret, when it seemed as if every other woman in Paris was stick-thin and ate only lettuce leaves and drank black coffee.

'I found a little bag of them in your handbag once.'

'You shouldn't have been looking through my things.'

'I was fetching your reading glasses for you, if you remember.'

She shook her head—an instinctive response, because all those little details that he'd lobbed at her like well-aimed missiles were making her realise how intimate her relationship with Leo really had been. She'd thought she'd kept her distance, armoured herself—the elegant Marguerite Ferrars, keeping their assignations in anonymous places. But in truth reality had seeped through. Emotion had too, as well as affection, with the glasses and the marshmallows and the cold feet. Little signs of how close they'd become, how much he'd begun to mean to her.

And she saw all too clearly how he would chip away at her defences now—how he would seduce her with knowing words and touches until she'd say yes. Of course she'd say yes. Because she was already more than halfway to loving him.

For a second—no more—Margo thought about actually accepting his proposal. Living a life she'd never thought to have, had made herself never want. A life of happiness but also of terrible risk. Risk of loss, of hurt, of heartbreak. Of coming apart so she'd never put the pieces of her soul back together again.

Reality returned in a cold rush and she shook her head. 'No, Leo.'

That faint smile had returned, although his eyes looked hard. 'Just like that?'

'Just like that.'

'You don't think I—*we*—deserve more explanation?'

'Not particularly.' She'd made her voice indifferent, maybe too much, because anger flashed in his eyes, turning the silver to grey.

He cocked his head, his gaze sweeping slowly over her. 'I think you're hiding something from me.'

She gave a scoffing laugh. 'You would.'

'What is that supposed to mean?'

'You can't believe I'm actually turning you down, can you?' The words tumbled out of her, fuelled by both anger and fear. 'You—the Lothario who has had half the single women in Europe.'

'I wouldn't go quite that far. Forty per cent, maybe.'

There was the charm, almost causing her to lose that needed edge of fury, to smile. 'No woman has ever resisted you.'

'You didn't,' he pointed out, with what Margo knew was deceptive mildness.

'Because I wanted a fling,' she declared defiantly. 'Sex without strings.'

'We never actually said—'

'Oh, but we did, Leo. Don't you remember that first conversation? We set out the rules right then.'

She saw a glimmer of acknowledgement in his eyes, and his mouth hardened into a thin line.

It had been an elaborate dance of words, their talk of

business concerns and obligations, veiled references to other places, other people—every careful remark setting out just what their affair would and wouldn't be. Both of them, Margo had thought, had been clear about their desire for a commitment-free relationship.

'I didn't think you wanted to get married,' she said.

Leo shrugged. 'I decided I did.'

'But you didn't at the beginning, when we met. You weren't interested then.' She'd felt his innate sense of distance and caution, the same as her own. They had, she'd thought, been speaking the same language, giving the code words for no commitment, no love, no fairytales.

'People change, Margo. I'm thirty-two. You're twenty-nine. Of course I'd think of settling down…starting a family.'

Something clanged hard inside her; she felt as if someone had pulled the chair out from under her and she'd fallen right onto the floor.

'Well, then, that's where we differ, Leo,' she stated, her voice thankfully cool. 'I don't want children.'

His eyebrows drew together at that. 'Ever?'

'Ever.'

He stared at her for a long, considering moment. 'You're scared.'

'Stop telling me what I feel,' she snapped, raising her voice to hide its tremble. 'And get over yourself. I'm not scared. I just don't want what you want. I don't want to marry you.' She took a breath, and then plunged on recklessly. 'I don't love you.'

He tensed slightly, almost as if her words had hurt him, and then he shrugged. 'I don't love *you*. But there are better bases for a marriage than that ephemeral emotion.'

'Such as?'

'Common goals—'

'How romantic you are,' she mocked.

'Did you want more romance? Would that have made a difference?'

'No!'

'Then I'm glad I didn't wine and dine you at Gavroche, as I was considering, and propose in front of a crowd.'

He spoke lightly enough, and yet she still heard an edge to his voice.

'So am I,' she answered, and held her ground as he took a step towards her. She could feel the heat rolling off him, felt herself instinctively sway towards him. She stopped herself, holding herself rigid, refusing to yield even in that small way.

'So this is it?' he said softly, his voice no more than a breath that feathered her face. His silvery gaze roved over her, seeming to steal right inside her. 'This is goodbye?'

'Yes.' She spoke firmly, but he must have seen something in her face, for he cupped her cheek, ran a thumb over her parted lips.

'You're so very sure?' he whispered, and she forced herself to stare at him, not to show anything in her face.

'Yes.'

He dropped his hand from her face to her breast, cupping its fullness, running his thumb over the taut peak. She shuddered; she couldn't help it. He'd always affected her that way, right from the beginning. A single, simple touch lit a flame inside her.

'You don't seem sure,' he murmured.

'We have chemistry, Leo, that's all.' She forced the words out past the desire that was sweeping through her, leaving nothing but need in its wake.

'Chemistry is a powerful thing.'

He slid his hand down to her waist, his fingers splaying across her hip. Sensation leapt to life inside her, low down, sparks shooting through her belly.

'It's not enough,' she said through gritted teeth.

She ached for him to move his hand lower, to touch her with the knowing expertise her body had once revelled in. Still she didn't move, and neither did Leo.

'Not enough?' he queried softly. 'So you want love, then?'

'Not with you.'

He stilled, and she made herself go on—say the words she knew would hurt them both and turn him from her for ever. She had to...she couldn't risk him breaking down any more of her defences. She couldn't risk, full stop.

'I don't love you, Leo, and I never will. Frankly, you were just a fling—something to while away the time. I never intended for it to be *serious*.' She let out a laugh, sharp and high, as Leo pulled back his hand from her hip. 'Honestly—a *proposal*?' She made herself continue. 'It's almost funny... Because I'd actually been planning to end it when we met in Rome next week.' She took a quick breath and went on recklessly. 'The truth is, I'm seeing someone else.'

He stared at her for a long, taut moment. A muscle flickered in his jaw, but that was all. 'How long?' he finally asked, the two words bitten off and spat out.

She shrugged. 'A couple of months.'

'*Months*—?'

'I didn't think we were exclusive.'

'I've always been faithful to you,' he said in a low voice.

'I never asked you to be,' she replied with another shrug.

She could hardly believe she was actually fooling him—didn't he see how she trembled? And yet she knew he was taken in. She saw it in the way everything in him had gone dangerously still.

Then a cold little smile played about his mouth.

'Well, then, this really is goodbye,' he said, and before she could answer he pulled her towards him and kissed her.

She hadn't been expecting it, the sudden press of his mouth on hers, knowing and sure, a delicious onslaught that had her insides flaring white-hot even as her mind scrambled frantically to resist.

But Leo had always been impossible to resist, and never more so than now, when he was utterly, ruthlessly determined to make her respond to him. His tongue slid inside her mouth as his hands spanned her waist, fitting her to his muscled body perfectly.

She kissed him back, gave herself up to the rush of sensations that left her dizzy with longing. The feel of Leo's hands on her body was so intense it almost hurt—like touching a raw nerve. He slid his hands under her tee shirt, discarding the flimsy bit of cotton with ease. And then her yoga pants were gone too. She kicked them off, needing to be naked, too enflamed by desire to feel either exposed or ashamed as she stood before him, utterly bare, her breath coming in pants and gulps.

Leo stood in front of her and slowly unbuttoned his shirt. She saw a predatory gleam in his eyes, but even that could not cool her desire. Was this his revenge? His punishment? Or simply his proof that she desired him still? Whatever it was, she'd take it. She'd welcome it. Because she knew it would be the last time she'd hold him in her arms, feel him inside her.

He shrugged his shirt off. The crisp white cotton slid off his shoulders, revealing his taut six-pack abs, the sprinkling of dark hair that veed towards his trousers. With a snick of leather he undid his belt and then kicked off his trousers, and he too was naked.

He came towards her, taking her in his arms in a way

that was possessive rather than sensual. When he kissed her she felt branded. Perhaps she always would.

He backed her towards the window, so her back was against the cold glass, and then without a single murmur or caress he drove inside her.

Even so she was ready for him, her body expanding to fit around his length. She wrapped her legs around his waist and pulled him inside her even more deeply, her head thrown back against the glass so she felt suspended between this world and the next, caught in a single moment of memory and desire.

The tension and pressure built inside her, a tornado that took over her senses, and at its dizzying peak Leo took her face in his hands and looked her straight in the eyes.

'You won't forget me,' he said, and it was a declaration of certainty, a curse, because she knew he was right.

Then, as her climax crashed over her, he shuddered into her and withdrew, leaving her trembling and weak-kneed against the window. She watched, dazed and numb, as he dressed silently. She could not form a single sentence, not even a word.

She watched him walk to the door. He didn't speak, didn't even look back. The door closed with a quiet, final-sounding click. Slowly she sank to the floor, clutching her knees to her chest as the aftershocks of her climax still shuddered through her.

Leo was gone.

CHAPTER TWO

LEO STRODE FROM Margo's apartment, his body still shuddering from their lovemaking—but no, he couldn't call it that. *Never* that.

With one abrupt movement he lobbed the little velvet box into the nearest bin. A foolish waste, perhaps, but he couldn't bear to look at that wretched ring for another moment. He couldn't stand the thought of it even being in his pocket.

He drew a deep breath and raked a hand through his hair, willing back the emotion that had nearly overwhelmed him in Margo's apartment. All of it. She was out of his life. He need never think of her again.

It wasn't as if he'd loved her, he reminded himself. Margo had been right about that. He had liked her, yes, and they'd certainly shared an explosive sexual chemistry. She'd seemed the obvious choice when he'd decided it was time he married.

Six months ago, just after their mother's death, his brother Antonios had resigned as CEO of Marakaios Enterprises and Leo had taken his place. It was what Leo had wanted his whole life, what he had striven for as a young man, working for the father who had never even noticed him. Who had chosen Antonios instead of him, again and again.

But he was over that; he'd made peace with Antonios, and his father had been dead for ten years. His mother too was gone now, and all of it together had made him want to marry, to start a family, create his own dynasty.

But Margo doesn't even want children.

Why hadn't he known that? Why hadn't he realised she was so faithless, so unscrupulous? *Theos*, she'd been *cheating* on him. He could hardly credit it; they'd seen each other every week or two at least, and their encounters had always been intense. But she had no reason to lie about such a thing.

And when he thought of how he'd asked her to marry him, how he'd tried to convince her, persuade her with gentle reason and understanding because he hadn't been able to believe she didn't want him… Leo closed his eyes, cringing with the shame of it.

Well, no more. He wouldn't marry. Or if he did it would simply be for a child. He would not engage his emotions, would not seek anything greater than the most basic of physical transactions. And he would never see Margo again, Margo of the cold feet and the marshmallows…

His face twisted with regret before he ironed out his features and strode on into the night.

Margo's stomach lurched for the third time that morning and she pressed one hand against her middle, closing her eyes and taking a deep breath. This stomach bug was both insistent and annoying. She'd been feeling nauseous for over a week, although she'd thankfully never actually been sick.

'Are you all right?'

Margo looked up to see Sophie, her colleague and fellow buyer at Paris's exclusive department store Achat, frowning at her.

They'd worked together for six years, starting as interns, Sophie with her freshly minted college degree and Margo doing it the hard way, having worked on the shop floor since she was sixteen. They'd both moved up to being assistants, and now they were buyers in their own right. Margo was in charge of the home department; Sophie covered accessories. Both of them were completely dedicated to their jobs.

'I'm fine. I've just been feeling a little sick lately.'

Sophie raised her eyebrows, a teasing smile playing about her mouth. 'If it was anyone but you I'd be worried.'

'What is *that* supposed to mean?' Margo asked, a note of irritability creeping into her voice. She had been out of sorts for a month now, ever since Leo had left her alone and aching.

It was for the best—it had to be—but she couldn't keep herself from feeling the hurt. The emptiness.

'I mean,' Sophie answered, 'that I'd think you were pregnant. But you can't be.'

'Of course I'm not,' Margo answered sharply.

Sophie knew her stance on relationships and children: one night over a bottle of wine they'd each confided their intention to have single, solitary, *safe* lives. At least that was how Margo had viewed it; she suspected Sophie just wanted to play the field.

'I'm on the mini-pill,' she stated, and Sophie raised her eyebrows.

'You haven't forgotten to take it, then?'

'No, never.'

Margo frowned at her computer screen and the image there of a selection of silk throw pillows, handcrafted in Turkey, that she was considering for Achat's exclusive range. Her mind was racing back to that night a month ago, when she and Leo had had their memorable farewell.

But she'd taken a pill that morning, and one the next day. She hadn't missed anything.

'Well, then, it's probably just a stomach bug,' Sophie said dismissively.

Margo barely heard her.

The next morning she'd taken it a bit later, she recalled. She hadn't been able to sleep after Leo had left, her mind seething and her body aching, so she'd taken a herbal sleeping tablet some time in the middle of the night. It had knocked her out, which had been a blessing at the time, and she had slept for eight hours, waking around eleven, which was only three hours after she normally took the pill…

She couldn't be pregnant.

But what if those few hours had made a difference? Allowed enough of a window…?

She let out a laugh, then, a trembling, near-hysterical sound that had Sophie looking up from her laptop across their shared open-plan office.

'Margo…?'

She shook her head. 'Just thinking how ridiculous your suggestion was.'

And then she turned back to her computer and worked steadily until lunchtime, refusing to give her friend's teasing suggestion a single second of thought.

Her mind was filled with a static-like white noise even as she focused on the Turkish pillows of hand-dyed silk, and at lunchtime she left her desk and hurried down the Champs-Élysées, walking ten blocks to a chemist that wasn't too close to Achat's offices.

She paced the length of the shop, making sure no one who knew her was inside, and then quickly bought a pregnancy test without meeting the cashier's eye. She stuck the paper bag in her handbag and hurried out of the shop.

Back at the office, she went into the bathroom, grateful that it was empty, and stared at her reflection, taking comfort from the elegant, composed face in the mirror. Her mask. Her armour. For work she wore nothing more than some eyeliner and red lipstick, a bit of powder. Her hair was in its usual sleek chignon and she wore a black pencil skirt and a silver-grey silk blouse.

The shade suddenly reminded her of the colour of Leo's eyes.

But she couldn't think about Leo now.

Taking a deep breath, she fumbled in her bag for the test and then locked herself in one of the stalls. She read the directions through twice, needing to be thorough, to focus on the details rather than the big picture that had been emerging ever since Sophie had made her suggestion.

Then she took the test and waited the requisite three minutes, staring at the face of her watch the whole time. As the second hand ticked to twelve for the third time she turned the test over—and stared down at two blazing pink lines.

Positive.

She was pregnant…with Leo's baby.

For a moment she couldn't think, couldn't breathe, couldn't even see. She doubled over as the world swam and darkened all around her. Then she took a few shallow breaths and straightened. She wrapped the test in a paper towel and shoved it deep in the bin, washed her hands and retouched her make-up. She would not think about this yet. She couldn't.

She went back to her office, ignoring a curious look from Sophie, and sat at her desk and worked non-stop until six. She took phone calls, she attended a meeting, she even chatted and joked a little with colleagues.

But all the time she could hear the buzzing in her head. She felt as if she were watching herself from a distance, applauding how effortlessly she was handling it all. Except she wasn't really…because inside she could feel the beginnings of panic ice over her mind and her belly.

She was pregnant with Leo's baby.

'Do you want to go for a drink?' Sophie asked as Margo rose to gather her things at six.

'I don't think…' Margo began, intending to put Sophie off, but then she hesitated.

She couldn't bear the thought of returning to her apartment and spending the evening alone—not with this bomb of knowledge still ticking inside of her, waiting to detonate.

'Why not?' she amended as lightly as she could, and slipped on her blazer.

It was a warm evening in early September, and the office buildings of Paris's centre were emptying out onto the wide boulevard of the Champs-Élysées. They walked to a wine bar on a narrow side street, one of their favourites, and sat outside at a rickety table so they could watch the world go by.

'Red or white?' Sophie asked as she moved to go inside and order their wine from the bar.

Margo hesitated, and then shook her head. 'I'll just have a glass of sparkling water. My stomach is still a little queasy.'

Sophie stared at her for a moment and Margo held the stare. She'd come out with Sophie tonight to avoid being home alone with this new knowledge, this new *life* inside her, but she wasn't ready to tell her friend yet.

'Very well,' Sophie said, and went inside.

Margo sat back in her chair and blindly watched people stream by, heading home or to a bar like this—people with plans, with jobs and busy lives…

Hours ago she'd been just like them—at least on the surface. To the world she presented an image of the confident, sophisticated career woman who had everything she wanted. She'd always known it was nothing more than a flimsy façade, but no one else had.

And now the façade was about to crumble. Because she was pregnant. Pregnant with a baby…a child of her own…

Instinctively her hand crept to her still flat stomach. She imagined the little life nestled inside her, the size of a grain of rice and yet with a brain and a beating heart. *A baby...*

'So what's going on?' Sophie asked as she returned to the table and handed Margo her glass of water.

Quickly Margo dropped her hand from her middle. 'What do you mean?'

'You've been acting strange all afternoon. Almost as if you were in a daze.'

'I've been working.'

Sophie just gave her a look; she knew her too well for Margo to dissemble. She took a sip of water to stall for time.

'Is everything all right?' Sophie asked quietly, abandoning her usual flippancy for a sincerity that made Margo's eyes sting.

She didn't have many friends. She had acquaintances and colleagues, people on the periphery of her life, but no one had ever been at its centre. She hadn't allowed anyone to be, because loneliness was safer. And maybe it was all she deserved.

If you'd married Leo he would have been there.

But she couldn't think that way because she'd made her choice. She couldn't change her mind now, couldn't wonder or wish for something else.

'Margo?' Sophie prompted, real concern wrinkling her forehead.

Margo took a deep breath. 'Actually…I really am pregnant.' She hadn't been planning on admitting it, but now that she had it was such a relief to share the burden, even if Sophie looked as dazed and shocked as she'd felt a few hours ago.

'Seriously? But…'

'I took a test at lunchtime.'

Sophie shook her head slowly. 'I didn't even know you were seeing anyone seriously.'

'I wasn't. It was…casual. He lives in Greece.'

'And…? Have you told him?'

Margo let out a trembling laugh. 'Sophie, I told you, I just found out at lunchtime.'

'Right.' Sophie sat back in her seat and took a sip of wine. 'So you're still processing it, I suppose?'

Margo passed a hand over her forehead. Telling Sophie had made her pregnancy seem more real, and she felt a bit shaky as a result. 'I don't think I've even started.'

'Well,' Sophie said, 'I didn't think you wanted children.'

'I didn't. Don't.'

Sophie raised an eyebrow and Margo realised her hand had strayed once more to her middle. She let out another uncertain laugh and dropped it.

'I don't know what I want,' she said quietly, and felt everything inside her lurch at this admission.

'What about the father, this Greek guy? How long had you been with him?'

'We were together for two years—'

'Two *years*?' Sophie's jaw dropped. 'Why didn't you ever *tell* me, Margo?'

'I…' Why *hadn't* she told Sophie about Leo? Because, she supposed, she had been afraid to allow Leo to seem that important to her, and yet she was afraid it had happened anyway. 'It was just a fling,' she said lamely.

Sophie laughed in disbelief. 'Quite a long-term fling.'

'Yes, I suppose… In any case, our…relationship is

finished. Completely.' Margo stared down at her glass of water. 'It didn't end well.'

'If you're thinking of keeping the baby, he should still know,' Sophie pointed out.

Margo couldn't keep herself from wincing. How on earth could she tell Leo now? Considering what she'd said to him the last time they'd been together, he might not even believe the baby was his.

'I can't think about all this just yet,' she said. 'It's too much. I have time.'

'If you're *not* going to keep it,' Sophie replied warningly, 'the sooner you decide the better. For your own sake.'

'Yes…'

A termination, she supposed, might seem like the obvious answer. And yet the most fundamental part of herself resisted the possibility, shrank away from it in horror.

She hadn't expected that. She hadn't expected pregnancy to awaken anything in her but dread and fear. And yet she couldn't deny the faint stirrings of hope, as ephemeral as a will-o'-the-wisp, that had gathered inside her. A *baby*. A second chance.

'You do have *some* time,' Sophie allowed, reaching over to pat her hand. 'Don't make any rash decisions, in any case.'

'I won't,' Margo promised, but already her mind was spinning, spinning. If she actually decided to keep the baby she would have to tell Leo. And how on earth would *that* work? Would he believe her? Would he want to be involved?

She left Sophie an hour later and took the Metro back to her apartment on the top floor of an eighteenth-century townhouse on the Île de la Cité. As she stepped into the little foyer, with its marble table and antique umbrella stand, she felt some of the tension leave her body, uncramp her shoulders. This was her home, her haven, lovingly created over the years and the only real one she'd ever known.

She ran a bubble bath in the claw-foot tub and sank gratefully into its warmth, closing her eyes and trying to empty her mind for a few moments. But thoughts crept stealthily back in. *A baby.* How would she manage with her job? Childcare in Paris was expensive, and she was entitled to only sixteen weeks of maternity leave. Even though she made a decent salary she didn't think she'd be able to keep her apartment *and* pay for the full-time childcare she'd need.

But far more concerning, far more terrifying than the financial implications of having a child, were the emotional ones. A baby…a human being she would be entirely responsible for, a person who would be utterly dependent on her…

A person she could love. A person she could lose. *Again.*

And then, of course, there was Leo. She didn't even know if he would see her or listen to anything she had to say. And if he did…would he want to be involved in her child's life? And if so…how much? How would they come to a custody arrangement? And was that what she wanted for her son or daughter? Some awful to-ing and fro-ing between parents who as good as hated each other?

Exhaustion crashed over her and she rose from the tub. She couldn't think about all this yet. She certainly couldn't come to any decisions.

As the days and then the weeks slipped past Margo knew she had to decide soon. Sophie had stopped asking her what she was going to do, but at work she could see the silent question in her friend's eyes and knew she was concerned.

And then the sickness really hit. The faint nausea that

had been plaguing her for a few weeks suddenly turned into something else entirely, something horrendous that left her barely able to get out of bed, and unable to keep anything down.

Lying alone in her bed, unable to do anything but crawl to the toilet, she realised how alone she was. She had so few friends in the city. Sophie wanted to help, but as a single working woman her resources and time were limited.

Margo knew all too well how short a step it was to destitution, to tragedy, when you were on your own. When there was no family, no safety net. If she was going to keep this baby she couldn't do it on her own. She couldn't risk it.

After suffering for a week, she managed to drag herself to the doctor for some anti-nausea medication.

'The good news,' the doctor told her cheerfully, 'is that nausea usually means a healthy pregnancy. That baby is here to stay.'

Margo stared at him, his words reverberating through her. He had no idea, of course, how conflicted she was about this child. Except in that moment she realised she wasn't conflicted at all. This baby was a gift—a gift she'd never expected to receive. And she knew then—realised she'd known all along—that of course she was keeping her child.

And of course she would have to tell Leo.

CHAPTER THREE

'SOMEONE'S HERE TO see you, sir.'

Leo glanced up from his laptop at his assistant Elena, who stood in the doorway of his office on the Marakaios estate. He'd been going over some figures for a new deal with a large North American restaurant chain, and it took a few seconds for Elena's words to penetrate.

'Someone? Who is it, Elena?'

'A woman. She wouldn't give her name, but she said it was urgent.'

Leo frowned. His office was on the family compound in central Greece—the middle of nowhere, as Margo had so acerbically reminded him. He didn't get unexpected visitors to his office here. *Ever.*

'Well, why on earth wouldn't she give her name?' he asked as he pushed back from his chair.

'I don't know. But she's well-dressed and well-spoken. I thought perhaps...'

Elena trailed off, blushing, and Leo took her meaning. She'd thought this woman might be one of his lovers. Only he hadn't taken a lover in months—not since he'd last seen Margo.

And he very much doubted *Margo* had come all the way to Greece to see him.

Leo's mouth twisted cynically at the thought. It had

been over four months since he'd seen her—over four months since he'd walked out of her apartment with that ring in his pocket. Four months since he'd let himself think of her. That part of his life was over.

'Whoever this woman is, Elena, I find it decidedly odd that she wouldn't give her name.'

'She seemed very insistent…'

With a sigh, Leo strode to the door. 'I'll see her, then,' he said, and walked briskly out of his office.

It wasn't until he reached the foyer and saw the woman standing there amidst the leather sofas and sleek coffee tables that his step slowed. His heart seemed to still. And an icy anger came over him like a frozen shell.

He folded his arms. 'If I'd known it was you I would have told Elena to send you away.'

'Please, Leo…' Margo said quietly.

She looked awful—gaunt, with dark shadows under her eyes. She wore a black wool coat that made her ivory skin look pale…too pale.

Leo frowned. 'What do you want?'

'To talk to you.' She glanced at Elena, who had gone back to her desk and was ostentatiously busying herself, but was of course listening to every word. 'Privately.'

Leo opened his mouth to tell her they had nothing to say to one another, but then he paused. He didn't want to have this conversation in public—didn't want anyone, even his assistant, to know his private affairs.

With a terse nod he indicated the corridor. 'Come to my office, then,' he said, and without waiting for her to follow he turned and strode back the way he had come.

He watched as Margo came in and carefully closed the door behind her. She looked bruised and exhausted, as if a breath of wind would knock her right over.

'You don't look very well,' he said flatly.

She turned to him with the ghost of a smile. 'I don't feel very well. Do you mind if I sit down?'

He indicated one of the two chairs in front of his desk and she sank into it with a sigh of weary relief.

'Well?' Leo asked, biting off the single syllable. 'What do you want?'

She looked up at him, and he felt a ripple of uneasy shock at the resignation in her eyes. It was so different from the way he'd usually seen her—all elegant polish and sassy sophistication. This was a different Margo… one with a layer stripped away.

'Leo,' she said quietly, 'I'm pregnant.'

He blinked, the words taking him totally by surprise.

She said nothing, waiting for his reply.

'And how does this concern *me*?' he asked coolly.

She held his iron gaze. 'The baby is yours.'

'And you know that *how*? Do I need to remind you of what you told me four months ago?'

'No.' She hesitated, her gaze moving away from his. 'The other…man…he can't be the father,' she said at last.

A rage so fierce it felt like an earthquake shaking his insides took hold of him. *'Don't,'* he said in a voice like a whip-crack, 'talk to me of him. *Ever.*'

'This baby is yours, Leo.'

'You can't know that.'

She sighed, leaning her head back against the chair. 'I *do* know it,' she said wearily. 'Utterly. But if you like I'll have a paternity test done. I can prove it beyond a doubt.'

He stared at her, shaken more than he wanted to admit or reveal that she sounded so certain. 'I thought you didn't want children,' he said, after a long, taut moment.

'I didn't,' she answered.

'Then I'm surprised you didn't just deal with this on your own,' he snapped.

She put a hand to her throat, the gesture making her seem even more fragile. Vulnerable.

'Is that what you would have wanted?'

'No.' He realised he meant it utterly. A child…*his* child, if she wasn't lying. Yet how could he trust a word she said? 'Why have you come here and told me?' he asked instead. 'Do you want money?'

'No, not particularly.'

He laughed at that—a cold, sharp sound. 'Not *particularly*?'

'I admit having this child will be hard for me financially. But I didn't come here to ask for a hand-out. I came because I thought you should know. You'd want to know.'

He sank into his chair, the reality of it crashing over him as he raked his hands through his hair. '*Theos*, Margo. This is a lot to take in.'

'I know. I've had three months to process it—'

'You've known for that long and you are only telling me *now*?'

Colour touched her cheeks faintly. 'I've been very ill. Extreme morning sickness, apparently.'

'Are you taking medication?' he asked sharply, and she nodded.

'It helps a little.' She sighed and shifted in her seat. 'The truth is, Leo, I didn't know how you would respond, or if you'd even see me. And I wanted to tell you in person. But with being so sick I couldn't face travelling all this way until now.'

He nodded. It all sounded so very reasonable and yet he still felt angry. He should have known. He should have had the choice to be involved from the beginning. And now…?

'If this is indeed my child,' he told her, laying his hands flat on the desk, 'there is no question of my not being involved.'

'I know.'

'And I don't mean some weekend arrangement,' Leo continued, knowing he meant it even though he was still reeling from her news. 'I won't be the kind of father who sees his child only on a Saturday afternoon.'

'No,' Margo agreed quietly. 'I don't want that either.'

'Don't you?'

He gazed at her narrowly for a moment. He still didn't understand why she was here. She hadn't possessed enough honour to be faithful to him, so why would she care whether he knew about his own child or not?

'I would have expected you to have had a termination,' he said abruptly. 'Or, if you wanted the child, to pass it off as this other man's.'

She winced at that. 'Clearly you don't have a very high opinion of me.'

'And you think I should?'

'No.' She let out a little defeated sigh. 'No, I don't.'

'So why didn't you do either of those things, Margo?'

It was the first time he'd said her name since he'd seen her again, and it caused him a sudden, surprising flash of pain. He clenched his hands into fists, then deliberately flattened them out, resting them again on his desk.

'Because I am not, no matter what you think, completely without morals,' she replied with a bit of her old spirit. 'I want my child, and I want my child to know its father.' She took a deep breath. 'And more than that I want my child to have a loving, stable home. A home where it knows it's safe, where its parents are, loving and protecting. *Always.*'

Her dark brown eyes seemed to glow with an inner fire, an utter conviction.

'And how,' Leo asked after a pause, 'do you suppose *that* is going to work?'

'That's the other thing I want,' Margo said, still holding his gaze, her eyes like burning coals in her pale face. 'I want you to marry me.'

In another situation, another life, Margo might have laughed at the way Leo's expression slackened with surprise. He hadn't been expecting that—and why would he? The last time he'd seen her she'd sent him away with a scornful rejection, told him lies of infidelity that she'd known would make him hate her. And here she was now, with a proposal of her own.

'You must,' Leo said, his voice like ice, 'be joking.'

'Do you think I'd come all the way to Greece just to make a joke?' Margo asked quietly.

Leo stood up, the movement abrupt. He paced in front of the window that overlooked the Marakaios olive groves, now stark and bare in winter, which produced Greece's finest olive oil.

'Your *proposal*,' he said, his teeth clenched and the word a sneer, 'is offensive.'

'I mean it sincerely—'

He cut her off, his voice now low and pulsating with fury. 'The last time I saw you, you told me you didn't want marriage or children.'

She gestured to the gently swelling bump that was just barely visible under her coat. 'Things have changed.'

'Not that much. Not for *me*.'

'Don't you want to know your own child?'

'Who says I won't? Who says I won't sue for custody?'

Her stomach plunged with fear at that, but she forced herself to stay calm.

'And do you think that would be in the best interest of our baby, Leo?'

He sat back down in his chair, raking his hands through

his hair. With his head lowered she could see the strangely vulnerable nape of his neck, the momentary slump of his shoulders, and everything in her ached.

'I'm sorry, Leo, for springing this on you,' she said quietly. 'I've thought long and hard over these last few months about what is best for our baby, and I've come to the conclusion that it's to live in a stable home with two parents.'

It hadn't been an easy decision to make, but Margo's own sorry history made her wary of going it alone as her mother had. Just like her, her mother had had no friends, no family, no safety net. And she'd lost everything.

Margo would not subject her child to the same risk.

He lifted his head, his eyes flashing although the set of his mouth was grim, bleak. 'Even two parents who don't love each other? Who have absolutely no reason whatsoever to respect or trust each other?'

She flinched slightly. 'I respect you, Leo.'

'You've had a funny way of showing it, then.'

She should tell him, Margo knew, that she'd made up the other man. Any hope of a marriage that was amicable at least was impossible with that perceived betrayal between them. But she was afraid Leo wouldn't believe her if she told him now, and even if he did believe her he would want to know why she had told such an outrageous and damaging lie. The answer to that question was to admit her own fear, and that was something she was not ready to do.

'I know you don't respect *me*,' she said.

She clenched her hands in her lap and fought another wave of nausea. The sickness had eased a bit in the last few weeks, but she still felt as if she had to drag herself through each day.

'I know you don't trust me. I hope that maybe, in time, I can win back both your respect and your trust. But this marriage would be for the sake of our child, Leo. To give our baby the opportunity of a stable home. And even if we don't love each other we'll both love this child.'

'So you're willing to enter a cold, loveless union, all for the sake of a baby you professed to not even want?'

Another deep breath and she met his gaze without a flinch. 'Yes.'

'I don't believe you.'

'Why would I be here, then?' she asked quietly.

'You want something. Are you in trouble? Did this other man throw you over? Do you need money?'

'I told you before, I'm not asking for a hand-out.'

'You also said,' Leo reminded her ruthlessly, 'that having this baby would be a struggle financially.'

'A struggle, yes, but not impossible. I could do it. I've thought about doing it,' she continued, determined to make him believe her, even if he didn't—*couldn't*—understand her motives. 'I thought very hard about raising this child on my own and not even telling you I was pregnant.'

'And yet you now want me to *trust* you?'

'I *didn't* choose to do that, Leo,' Margo said, her voice rising. She strove to level it; giving in to temper now would not help her cause. 'I knew that you needed to know, and that our child needed more. Two parents. Stability, safety—'

'You don't think you could give this child those things on your own?'

'No. Not for certain. I don't...I don't have a lot of friends, and no family. This baby needs more than just me. He or she needs a father.'

'If I *am* the father.'

'Please...'

She closed her eyes, waves of both nausea and fatigue crashing over here. Coming all this way, dealing with the plane and the rental car and the endless travel, had completely exhausted her.

She summoned what little strength she had left and made herself continue. 'Let's not argue. I want to marry you for the sake of our child. I'm not expecting you to love me or even like me after—after what I did, but I do hope we might act amicably towards each other for the sake of the baby. As for…' She dropped her gaze, unable to look him in the eye. 'As for the usual benefits of a marriage… I'd understand if you chose to look elsewhere.'

Leo was silent and Margo risked a look up, wondering if he'd taken her meaning.

'Am I to understand,' he asked, his voice toneless, 'that you are giving me permission to violate my marriage vows?'

'It would be a marriage of convenience—'

'But still a marriage.'

'I'm trying to make this more amenable to you—'

'To sweeten the deal?' He cut across her, his voice hard. 'It still tastes rancid to me.'

'Please, Leo…' She swallowed, hating the fact that she had to beg.

Maybe he was right. Perhaps she should go back to Paris, raise the baby on her own. Leo could be the sort of weekend father he claimed he didn't want to be. Plenty of couples did it—why not them?

Because she was afraid of going it alone. Because she wanted more for her child. So much more than she'd had.

'You ask so *nicely*,' Leo said, his eyes glittering now.

He was furious with her, even after so many months apart. She wondered if his anger could ever be appeased. Perhaps if she told him the truth…if only he would believe it.

'I'm willing to live in Greece,' she continued, deciding she might as well say it all.

'Even in the "middle of nowhere"?'

'I'd leave my job at Achat. I'd want to stay home with the baby for the first few years, at least.'

'I thought the whole "housewife routine" bored you to death?'

Once again he was throwing her words back in her face, and she couldn't blame him. 'It's different now.'

'So you're saying you *want* those things? That life?'

He sounded incredulous—contemptuous, even—and bile surged in her stomach again. She swallowed past the metallic taste in her mouth. 'I'm saying that I am willing,' she answered. 'It's a sacrifice I'm prepared to make.'

'So I'd be marrying a martyr? What an appealing thought.'

'You'd be making a sacrifice too,' Margo replied. 'I understand that.'

'I still don't understand you,' Leo answered.

'Why is it so hard to believe I'd be willing to do this?' Margo demanded. She could take only so much of his sneering disbelief. 'Most women would.'

'And yet,' Leo reminded her softly, 'you *aren't* "most women".'

She closed her eyes, felt herself sway.

She heard Leo's sharply indrawn breath. 'Margo, are you all right?'

His voice was rough, although with impatience or anxiety she couldn't tell.

She forced her eyes open.

'I'm just very tired, and still quite nauseous,' she said levelly. 'Obviously you need time to think about my—my proposal.' Not the word she'd wished to use, and Leo's mouth twisted cynically when she said it. There had been too many proposals already. 'If you could let me know when you've decided…'

'Are you actually intending to return to France?' Leo asked sharply. 'You're in no condition to travel.'

'I'll spend the night at a local hotel,' she answered, 'and fly out of Athens tomorrow.'

'No.' Leo's gaze was cold and implacable as he gave his order. 'You'll stay here. I'll give you my answer tomorrow.'

Which made her feel like Scheherazade, wondering if she was to be beheaded in the morning. Not the way she would have wanted to think about her marriage, but she'd reconciled herself, or thought she had, to what life with Leo would be like. She'd told herself it was worth it, that anything was worth it if she could give her baby a stable, loving home.

Even if you and Leo will never love each other?

Some sacrifices, she reminded herself grimly, were necessary. And maybe it would be better this way. Without the complication and risk of loving someone, you could never be hurt. Hopefully.

She rose from her chair, blinking back dizziness. Even so Leo must have seen something in her expression, for he reached forward and steadied her elbow with his hand. It was the first time he'd touched her in three months, since he'd made love to her against the window and then walked away.

'I'm fine,' she said, and shook off his hand. 'Just a little dizzy when I stand up, that's all.'

'I'll arrange for someone to show you to the guest suite,' Leo said.

He was frowning, although over her dizziness or the whole situation she didn't know. Couldn't think. He was right: she really wasn't in a fit state to travel.

She stood, swaying slightly, as Leo made arrangements on his phone. Then he ended the call and gave her one last, hard look.

'I'll see you tomorrow,' he said, and Margo knew it was a dismissal.

CHAPTER FOUR

A baby. He was going to be a father… If the child was truly his. Leo knocked back his third whisky and stared grimly out at the starless night. It had been eight hours since Margo had confronted him in his office, and he was still reeling.

He hadn't seen her in all that time. Elena had taken her to the house, and then his personal staff had seen to her comforts. He'd called his housekeeper Maria to check on her, and she'd told him that Margo had gone to her room and slept for most of the afternoon. He'd requested that a dinner tray be taken up to her, but Maria had told him it hadn't been touched.

Anxiety touched with anger gnawed at his gut. If the child was his, he wanted to make sure Margo was staying healthy. Hell, even if the child *wasn't* his, he had a responsibility towards any person under his roof. And he hadn't liked how pale and ill Margo had looked, as if the very life force had been sucked right out of her.

Restlessly Leo rose from the leather club chair where he'd been sitting in the study that had once been his father's, and then his brother Antonios's. And now it was his. Six months into his leadership of Marakaios Enterprises and he still burned with the determination to take the company to a new level, to wield the power his father and brother had denied him for so long.

A lifetime of being pushed to the sidelines, being kept in the dark, had taken its toll. He didn't trust anyone—and especially not Margo. But if the child was his…then why *not* the cold marriage of convenience she'd suggested? It was what he'd determined he'd wanted after she'd turned him down. No messy emotion, no desperate searching for love. He just hadn't expected Margo to be his convenient bride.

Grimly Leo turned back to the whisky bottle. What she'd suggested made sense, and yet everything in him resisted it. To live with a woman who had been unfaithful, who had *rejected* him, and who was now viewing their marriage as the altar upon which she'd sacrifice herself, her hopes and dreams… It was a bitter pill to swallow—and yet what was the alternative? To come to some unsatisfactory custody arrangement and not be nearly as involved in his child's life as he wanted?

If the child was his.

If it was then Leo knew he had to be involved. He wanted to be the kind of father his own father hadn't been to him. Loving, interested, open. And he wanted a family—a child, a wife. Why not Margo? He could control his feelings for her. He had no interest in loving her any more.

He could make this marriage work.

Margo had thought she wouldn't be able to sleep, but she was so tired that she'd fallen into a deep and thankfully dreamless sleep the moment her head had hit the pillow, after Leo's housekeeper had shown her to her room.

When she awoke it was dark and the room was chilly, the curtains open to the night sky. Margo rolled over in bed, feeling disorientated and muzzy-headed, as if she were suffering from jet lag or a hangover, or both. She heard a knock on the door, an urgent *rat-a-tat-tat* that made her think it was not the first knock.

She rose from the bed, pushing her hair out of her face, and went to answer the door.

The housekeeper Maria stood there, with a tray of food. The salad, bread, and lentil soup looked and smelled delicious, but Margo's stomach roiled all the same. She didn't think she could manage a mouthful.

'*Efharisto*,' she murmured, and reached out to take the tray.

But Maria would have none of it. She shook her head and bustled into the room, setting the tray on a table in the corner. Bemused, Margo watched as she drew the curtains across the windows and remade the bed, plumping the pillows. She turned on a few table lamps that were scattered about the room and then looked around, seemingly satisfied with how cosy she'd made it in just a few minutes.

'*Efharisto*,' Margo said again, and Maria nodded towards the food.

'*Fae*,' she commanded, and while Margo didn't recognise the word she could guess what it meant. *Eat*.

She gave the housekeeper a weak smile and with another nod Maria left the room.

Margo walked over to the tray and took a spoonful of soup, but, warm and nourishing as it was, her stomach roiled again and she left it.

Now that the cobwebs were clearing from her brain she remembered every excruciating detail of her conversation with Leo. His disbelief and his contempt, his suspicion and anger. And now she was stuck here, waiting to see if he would marry her.

Shaking her head at her own stubborn folly, she crawled back into the bed and pulled the covers over herself. She wouldn't back out of her offer. She cared too much about this child inside her—this child she'd never expected to have, never dared want.

This child she would sacrifice anything for to ensure it had a better childhood, a better life, than she had had. To keep her, or him, safe.

She slept again and when she woke it was dawn, with the first grey light of morning creeping through a crack in the closed curtains. She dozed for a little while longer and then finally got up and went to shower, to prepare herself to meet with Leo and hear his answer—whatever it was.

At eight o'clock Maria knocked on the door and brought in a breakfast tray. Margo didn't know whether to feel like a pampered princess or a prisoner. At some point, she realised, Maria must have removed the untouched tray from the night before. She must have been sleeping at the time.

'*Efharisto*,' she said again, and Maria gave her a stern look.

'*Fae*.'

'Yes—I mean, *ne*.' Margo smiled apologetically. 'I can't keep much down, I'm afraid.'

Maria clucked at that, but Margo didn't think the older woman understood her. She bustled about a bit more, pouring coffee and juice, taking the lids off jam and butter dishes. Finally she left and Margo gazed in dismay at the lavish breakfast Maria had left. The smell of the coffee made her stomach lurch.

For the housekeeper's sake she tried to eat some yogurt with honey, but after two spoonsful she left it aside and then paced the room, wondering if she should go in search of Leo or wait for him to summon her.

She'd paced for several minutes, restless and anxious, until she realised she was being ridiculous. Had she lost all her spirit since coming here? She might be tired and unwell, and afraid of Leo's response, but she'd faced far worse obstacles than this and survived. Her strength in the face of adversity was something she clung to and prided herself on.

Determinedly she strode to the door and flung it open—only to stop in her tracks when she saw Leo standing there, looking devastatingly handsome in a crisp white shirt and grey trousers, his ink-dark hair still damp and spiky from a shower. He also looked decidedly nonplussed.

'Going somewhere?' he enquired.

'Looking for you, actually,' she replied crisply. 'I'd like your answer, Leo, because I need to get back to Paris. My flight is at two o'clock this afternoon.'

'Cancel it,' he returned. 'You won't be returning to Paris. Not right now, at any rate.'

She stared at him, as nonplussed as he'd been. 'Excuse me?'

His eyes flashed and his mouth thinned. 'Which part of what I said didn't you understand?'

Margo gritted her teeth. Yesterday she might have donned a hair shirt and beaten her chest in grief and repentance, but clearly that hadn't been enough for Leo. She didn't think she could endure a lifetime of snide remarks, all for a crime she hadn't even committed.

Except you told him you did.

'Perhaps,' she suggested, with only a hint of sharpness, 'we could discuss our future plans in a bit more detail?'

'Fine. I was coming to get you, anyway. We can go down to my study.'

'Fine.'

Silently she followed him down the terracotta-tiled corridor to the sweeping double staircase that led to the villa's soaring entrance hall. Yesterday she'd been too overwhelmed and exhausted to take in any of her surroundings, but today she was keenly aware that this grand place was, in all likelihood, her new home. It seemed, based on what Leo had said about cancelling her flight, that he was going to agree to marry her.

And from the plunging sensation in her stomach she knew she wasn't sure how she felt about that.

He led her to a wood-panelled study overlooking the villa's extensive gardens. This late in November they were stark and bare, but Margo could imagine how lush and lovely they would be come spring. Would she walk with her baby out there? Bring a blanket and lie on the grass, look up at the clouds while the baby gurgled and grabbed its feet?

'Let me cut to the chase,' Leo said, and Margo was jolted out of her pleasant daydream to the current cold reality.

He stood behind a huge desk of carved mahogany, his hands braced on the back of a chair, his expression implacable.

In the two years they'd been together she'd seen his lazy, knowing smiles, his hooded sleepy gazes. She'd seen him light and laughing, and dangerously, sensually intent. But she hadn't seen him like this—looking at her as if she were a difficult business client.

Well, if he could be businesslike, then so could she. She straightened and gave him a brisk nod. 'Please do.'

'I will marry you—but only on certain conditions.'

Margo took a deep breath and let it out evenly. 'Which are?'

'First, we drive to Athens this afternoon and you undergo a paternity test.'

It was no more than she'd expected, although the fact that he believed the baby might not be his still stung. This, at least, was easy to comply with. 'Very well.'

'Second, you resign from your job immediately and come and live with me here in Greece.'

So he wanted complete control of her and their child? She couldn't say she was really surprised. 'Fine.'

'Third, you agree to have a local doctor of my choosing provide you with medical care.'

Her temper finally started to fray. 'I think I'm capable of finding my own doctor, Leo.'

'Are you?' He arched an eyebrow, coldly sceptical. 'Because you came here looking dreadful.'

'Thanks very much, but my looks have nothing to do with my medical care or lack of it,' Margo snapped.

How much of this was she supposed to take? Maybe, she thought with a surge of reckless fury, the answer was none of it. She'd come to Leo as a supplicant, truly believing that their child should know his or her father. Trusting that she was making the right decision in seeking to provide the kind of stable home life she'd never had…no matter what the sacrifice to her.

If Leo was going to snipe at her constantly, was that really an environment she wanted to raise her child in? The kind of relationship she wanted her son or daughter to emulate?

But the alternative was too bleak to consider. Raise her baby alone, a single mother without a safety net. No parents, no relatives, no one who could help or support her besides a few friends like Sophie, who didn't even want children themselves. One wrong choice or an accident away from destitution, from losing everything. *Again.*

'Leo,' she said, keeping her voice even, 'if you're going to snipe at me about everything this whole negotiation process will be very unpleasant.'

Leo's mouth hardened. 'I'm just trying to be clear.'

'You are. Abundantly.'

A muscle flickered in his jaw. His gaze was the colour

of a sea in winter, slate-grey and utterly icy. 'I'm not finished with my conditions.'

'Fine,' she said wearily. 'What are the rest of your conditions?'

'You don't work while you're pregnant—or while our child is small. I want my child to have a mother who is fully present and available.'

'I've already said I would give up my job for a few years,' she reminded him. 'And anyway, considering I'll be stuck in the middle of Greece, a career is hardly an option for me at the moment.'

'Our marriage might be made for convenience,' Leo continued relentlessly, 'but it won't be *that* convenient. When you are healthy, and recovered from the birth of our child, I want you in my bed.'

Her stomach plunged again, with that weird mixture of anticipation and dread. 'I thought you could hardly stand the sight of me?' she said after a second's pause. Her voice sounded husky.

'We have chemistry,' Leo answered. 'Why should I look elsewhere when I have a woman to see to my needs right there at home?'

'Are you *trying* to be as offensive as possible?'

'Just stating facts,' Leo answered in a bland voice. 'And here's another fact: if you ever cheat on me again I will divorce you. Immediately. And I will gain complete custody of our child.'

Margo stared at him for a moment, saw the steely glint of challenge in his eyes, the hard set of his mouth.

Her hands clenched into fists at her sides. 'No.'

'No? You mean you can't even *pretend* you're going to be faithful?'

'I'll be faithful to you, Leo,' Margo said, her voice very even despite the maelstrom of fury and pain she felt whirling through her. 'But if you ever threaten to take my child away from me again I will leave you and I will never come back. I will go where you will never find me, and you will never see either of us again—' She broke off, her nails digging into her palms, her chest heaving.

'That's a lot of nevers,' Leo remarked tonelessly.

'You started it.'

'I wonder why you are so fierce and protective,' he answered, his silvery gaze sweeping slowly over her, 'when you made it abundantly clear the last time we met that you didn't even *want* children.'

'People change.'

'And yet I wonder if you really have?'

She shook her head, her anger subsiding, replaced only by weariness. She sank onto one of the chairs in front of his desk. 'Are there any other conditions?'

'None we need to discuss at present.'

She looked up. 'Good. Then I have a few of my own.'

She almost laughed at the look of shock that blazed across his features. Did he think her so weak and spineless that she would accept all his conditions without naming her own? Or perhaps he was simply that confident of his own strong position.

She thought of his threat—no, his *promise* to claim full custody if she was unfaithful, or even if he just thought she was unfaithful. His position was strong and hers was weak, because she knew her threat to leave him and go where he could never find her was just that: a threat. Empty. Meaningless.

Leo would always find her.

'So what are your conditions?' he asked, folding his arms.

'First, that you never threaten me again.' She glared at him and he gazed back, unsmiling.

'What you call "threat" I call statement of fact.'

'Nevertheless.'

He shrugged. 'What are the others?'

Margo almost dug her heels in and argued the point, but she was so very, very tired. 'I have sole care of our child. No nannies or nurses.'

He inclined his head in acknowledgement. 'You'll have no argument from me. I said I wanted you to be present and available.'

'Even though you don't respect or trust me?' Margo couldn't help but jibe.

Leo pressed his lips together, and then bit out, 'I trust you to be a good mother to our child.'

And despite all his sneers and orders it touched her that he thought that. Because the truth was she wasn't sure she thought it herself. She *wanted* to be a good mother, God knew, but she certainly hadn't had the best example. And she had too many regrets when it came to loving a child. Losing a child.

'What else?' Leo asked.

'Any decisions regarding our child's welfare are made jointly. I won't have you laying down the law when it comes to our baby.'

His jaw set. 'It seems reasonable to discuss things,' he said after a pause.

Margo cast around for more conditions, but she couldn't think of anything. This was all so unknown, so unbelievable. She had no idea what her marriage, her *life* would look like. *But at least it would be safe.* Her baby would be safe.

'Good,' she said finally, with a nod. 'Then I have no more conditions…at present.'

'I'm glad we've come to an agreement,' Leo answered, inclining his head. 'We'll leave for Athens this afternoon.'

'I will have to return to France at some point,' Margo warned him. 'I have to give notice and deal with my apartment.'

She swallowed, the realisation of all she was leaving behind hitting her with sudden force, making her breathless. The career she was so proud of. The friends she'd made. The home she'd created for herself—her sanctuary and haven, the only place she felt she could be herself. All of it gone.

But it's worth it. It has to be worth it.

'When you are fit to travel,' Leo said, his tone implying that *he* would be the one to make the decision, 'you may return to France and deal with your job and apartment.'

His imperious tone, as if he were giving her permission, grated on Margo's already raw nerves. 'Who do you think you are,' she demanded, 'to order me about in such a way? I *chose* to come here, Leo—'

'I'll tell you who I am,' Leo cut across her, his voice quiet and deadly. 'I'm your husband.'

'Not yet,' Margo answered, her voice just as quiet, just as deadly. 'And at the rate you're going maybe not ever.'

He took a step towards her, his eyes narrowing to silver slits. 'Do you *really* think,' he asked, 'that I'd let you go now you are carrying my child? *If* it is my child.'

'Oh, enough with that, Leo—'

'We'll know the truth by tomorrow,' he answered. 'And then we'll be married.'

CHAPTER FIVE

THEY DIDN'T SPEAK during the three-hour drive to Athens. His hands clenched on the wheel, Leo slid a covert, sideways glance towards Margo. She sat very still, one hand resting on the handle of the door, her face pale and composed.

She seemed a little better than she had yesterday, but she still looked tired and washed out. She wore a sweater dress of magenta wool that clung to her shape, making him realise just how much weight she'd lost—although he could still see the gentle swell of her small baby bump. *His* baby.

He was, of course, going to insist on the paternity test, and yet Leo felt in his gut that the baby was his. Margo wouldn't have agreed to everything so readily if she'd had any doubt. Which made him wonder how she could be so certain.

He hadn't given much thought to the other man in Margo's life; he'd simply shut the door on the whole idea and tried not to think of her—or him—at all. Now, however, he wondered—and he realised they needed to address it.

'This other man,' he said abruptly. 'Are you still with him?'

She turned to him, the ghost of a sad smile curving her lips. 'Do you think I'd be here if I was?'

'I have no idea.'

She let out a small sigh. 'No, Leo. We're not together.'

'When did you break it off?'

She didn't answer and his hands clenched harder on the steering wheel, his knuckles turning white.

'Well, Margo? It's not that hard a question. I need to know if this guy is going to resurface in our lives, because I assure you—'

'Oh, this is ridiculous,' she said, and closed her eyes. 'Leo, there *is* no other man. There never was.'

He turned sharply to stare at her. Her eyes were still closed; she was leaning her head back against the seat. 'You expect me to believe that?'

'Not really, but it's the truth.'

'Why did you lie to me before, then?' he demanded.

Again she didn't answer, and he wondered if she were scrambling for some plausible excuse.

'Because,' she finally said softly, her eyes still closed, 'I knew it was the one thing that would send you away for good.'

Leo blinked, stung by this almost as much as he'd been by her alleged infidelity. 'You mean my proposal of marriage was so abhorrent to you that you needed to *lie* to get rid of me?'

'You're putting it in the worst possible light, but, yes, I suppose that's true.'

The sheer rejection of it, as brutal as his father's had been, left him speechless.

He stared straight ahead, flexing his hands on the steering wheel. 'And yet here we are, about to get married.'

She opened her eyes and gazed at him bleakly. 'Yes. Here we are.'

'I don't understand you, Margo.'

'I know.'

'If, four months ago, the idea of marrying me was so

disagreeable, why did you come back? Plenty of children live with single or divorced parents. You could have managed. I wouldn't have forced you to marry me. We could have come to a custody arrangement.' He hesitated, and then continued. 'We still could.'

'Is that what you want?'

'I don't know.' He shook his head, thoughts whirling through his mind like leaves in an autumn wind. Margo's rejection of him hurt more than he wanted to admit. And yet…she'd come back. She'd chosen to be here. They could still find a way ahead, for the sake of their child.

And the truth is, you still want her.

Underneath his anger the old desire burned just as bright, just as fierce.

'Leo…there's no reason we can't be amicable with each other, is there?'

She laid her hand on his arm, her fingers long and slender, the touch as light as a butterfly and yet still seeming to reach right inside him and clench a fist around his heart.

'We can be friends,' she continued. 'A convenient marriage doesn't have to be a cold one.'

Friends—when she'd either cheated on him or lied in the worst possible way in order to avoid marrying him? Friends—when she clearly viewed marriage to him as a *sacrifice*? The desire he'd felt was no more than that: desire. Lust.

He pulled his arm away. 'I don't think so,' he answered coolly. 'I think it's best if we keep this businesslike.'

She turned her head towards the window. 'And will we be "businesslike" in bed?'

'We've never had a problem with that aspect of our relationship,' Leo answered. He'd keep his physical feelings for Margo separate from any potential emotional complications. 'And we won't once we're married.'

They were on the outskirts of Athens now, with the raised mount of the Acropolis visible on the horizon. They didn't speak until they'd reached Leo's apartment in Kolonaki.

Margo had never been to Leo's city home before. Now she walked around the elegant rooms that took up the top floor of a nineteenth-century townhouse. The living room and dining room had been knocked together to create a large open space scattered with black and white leather sofas and tables of chrome and glass.

A huge canvas of wavy green lines and white splotches was the only colour in the whole room. She stood in front of it, wondering if this was the kind of modern art Leo liked. It had probably cost a fortune, and it looked as if it had been painted by a five-year-old.

'A masterpiece made by my nephew Timon,' he said as he came to stand beside her.

'I didn't know you had a nephew.'

There was, she realised, so much she didn't know about him. She knew what he liked in bed, and what kind of food he liked to order in, and that he preferred classical music to jazz. She knew he shaved with an old-fashioned straight razor and that the only cologne he wore was a splash of citrus-scented aftershave. She knew what a woman would know of a lover, but not of someone she loved. Not of a husband.

'Yes, my sister's son.'

'Is he an aspiring artist, then?' she asked, with a nod to the canvas.

'I suppose you could say that. He's three.'

Margo let out a surprised laugh. 'And I was just thinking this painting looked like it was done by a five-year-old and had probably cost a fortune.'

'Luckily for me, it cost nothing. My interior designer wanted me to spend a hundred thousand euros on some modern atrocity and I said my nephew could do something better. He did.' He glanced briefly at the huge canvas. 'I quite like it, actually. It's meant to be the olive groves, when the trees blossom in spring.'

'I like it too,' Margo answered. 'Especially now that I know it's done by your nephew.'

For a moment, no more, it felt like the way things had used to be, or even better. Easy, relaxed… A faint smile curved Leo's mouth as he stared at the painting, and Margo felt her wilting spirits lift as hope that they might in fact be able to have an amicable marriage after all unfurled inside her.

Then Leo turned away.

'I've put your things in the guest bedroom. You can refresh yourself and then we'll go to the doctor.'

The guest bedroom was as sumptuous as the rest of the apartment, with a huge king-sized bed covered in a cream silk duvet and an en-suite bathroom with a sunken marble tub. Margo was tempted to run a bath and have a soak, but she knew Leo would be waiting, watching her every move, and the thought made her too uptight to relax, even in a bubble bath.

She washed her face and hands instead, and put on a little make-up, no more than concealer to cover the dark shadows under her eyes, and a little blusher and lipstick to give her face some colour.

'Have you eaten today?' Leo called through the closed door. 'Maria told me you didn't have supper last night, nor breakfast this morning.'

So Maria was her keeper and his spy? Margo tried not to let it rankle. 'I can't manage much food,' she answered. She took a quick breath and opened the door.

Leo stood there, scowling.

'You need to keep up your strength.'

'I would if I could, Leo, but I can't keep anything down.'

'I thought the medication you were prescribed helps?'

'It does,' Margo answered. 'But I still have to be careful.' She tried for a smile. 'I've eaten a lot of melba toast. It's the one thing my stomach can stand.'

'Melba toast?' he repeated.

Margo shrugged. 'My doctor said I should start to feel better soon.'

'I don't even know how far along you are.'

'Seventeen weeks. The baby is due in the end of April.'

He looked startled by that news, and Margo wondered if the actuality of a baby—a living person coming into their lives—had just become more real to him.

But all he said was, 'We should go.'

'I'll just get my coat.'

Leo insisted on driving to the doctor's, even though it was only a few blocks away.

'You look as if a breath of wind could knock you over,' he informed her, and Margo told herself he was actually being considerate, even if it came across, as did everything else, as both a command and a criticism.

The doctor's office was plush and well-appointed, and they were seen immediately. Margo perched on top of the examination table, feeling shy and rather exposed with Leo in the room, standing in the corner, practically glowering.

The doctor, a neat-looking woman with a coil of dark hair and a brisk, efficient manner, took them both in with a single glance. 'Would you prefer to be seen alone?' she asked Margo in clipped English.

Leo looked taken aback. Clearly he'd expected the doctor he'd chosen to leap to do his bidding, just as everyone else did.

'No,' Margo answered, 'but maybe you could sit down?' She raised her eyebrows at Leo, who took a seat without a word.

'Now, let's see.' The woman, who had introduced herself as Dr Tallos, flipped through the forms Margo had filled out in the waiting room. 'You believe you're seventeen weeks along? Have you had an ultrasound?'

'Not yet. I was scheduled for one at twenty weeks.'

'Well, we can do one now, just to make sure everything's all right,' Dr Tallos said briskly. 'If you'd like?'

A tremor of both fear and excitement rippled through Margo. 'Yes, all right.'

'Let's get that done first, then, shall we?'

'What about the paternity test?' Leo asked, and the doctor shot him a narrowed look while Margo flushed at the obvious implication.

'We can establish paternity by a simple blood test. I'll draw blood from both of you after we've established the baby is healthy.' She raised her eyebrows at him, her expression and voice both decidedly cool. 'If that's all right with you?'

A blush touched Leo's cheeks and Margo almost felt sorry for him. The doctor didn't know their convoluted history.

'That's fine,' he said, and sat back in his chair.

A nurse wheeled in a machine with a screen and wires, and Margo lay back on the examination table.

'Do you mind?' Dr Tallos asked, and lifted her dress all the way up to right underneath her breasts, pulling her tights down to reveal the soft white swell of her belly.

Now she felt really exposed, lying there like a beached whale with her belly on view. She couldn't so much as sneak a glance at Leo, but she felt his presence, his tension.

'This will be a little cold,' Dr Tallos murmured, and squirted a clear gel onto Margo's bare stomach.

It wasn't just cold, it was icy, and she shivered.

'Here we go.' She started pressing a wand into Margo's belly, hard enough to make her wince.

'That's hurting her,' Leo said sharply, and both Margo and Dr Tallos turned to him in surprise.

'It's a bit uncomfortable,' the doctor said, 'but I promise you it's not hurting anyone.'

Leo didn't look convinced, and Margo said quietly, 'I'm all right, Leo.'

'There we are,' Dr Tallos announced, and they all turned to look at the fuzzy shape on the screen.

Margo blinked, trying to connect what looked like nothing more than a few blobby circles into a shape that resembled a baby.

Then Dr Tallos started pointing things out on the screen. 'There's the head, and the stomach, and you can see fingers and toes—look.'

And almost as if by magic Margo could see it: the curled up bud of her baby unfurling as he—or she—stretched out arms, kicked tiny legs.

'Kicking up a storm,' Dr Tallos said cheerfully. 'Do you feel anything?'

Margo shook her head. 'Not yet.'

'Well, don't worry, you're sure to in the next few weeks. And there's the heart, beating away.' She pointed to the flickering image on the screen, pulsing with life. 'Let me turn up the volume and you can hear it.'

She twirled a knob on the ultrasound machine and all at once the room was filled with a sound like the galloping of a horse, an insistent swoosh that had both Leo and Margo's jaws dropping in amazement.

'I've never heard such a sound,' Leo said softly.

He looked gobsmacked, as if someone had hit him on the head, and Margo knew how he felt. That rushing sound had knocked her for six too. It was so *real*.

'Baby is measuring seventeen weeks, just as you said,' Dr Tallos continued as she pressed some keys to take measurements. 'Everything looks well. It's a bit early to tell the sex, but we'll schedule a more comprehensive ultrasound for twenty weeks. Now…' She flicked off the machine and removed the wand from Margo's stomach before handing her a paper towel to wipe off the gel. 'I'll give you a moment to clean yourself and we'll do the blood test.' She turned to Leo with raised eyebrows. 'I'm assuming that's still required?'

He hesitated, and Margo jumped in. 'Yes, it's required,' she said. She would not have Leo casting any more aspersions or doubt.

Fifteen minutes later they'd left the doctor's office, with their promise to call with the results of the paternity test tomorrow.

It was strange, walking along the city street together, crossing the wide boulevard lined with cafés and upscale boutiques.

'Wait just a moment,' Leo said, and ducked into a gourmet deli.

Margo waited on the pavement, the brisk December wind buffeting her.

He came out a few minutes later, a paper bag in hand. 'Melba toast,' he said, and Margo, quite suddenly, felt near to tears. 'Margo, what is it?' he asked.

She sniffed and shook her head. 'Nothing. I'm just emotional because I'm pregnant. And being at the doctor's office…hearing the heartbeat…'

Leo frowned. 'That was a good thing, was it not?'

'Yes. Yes, of course it was.'

And yet hearing that heartbeat had also terrified her—because what if it stopped? What if the next time she had an ultrasound she heard nothing but yawning, endless silence? She was used to expecting, and experiencing, the worst. She couldn't bear for it to happen again, and yet she still braced herself for it.

'Here.' Leo opened the bag of melba toast and handed her a piece. 'Eat something. You'll feel better.'

But his kindness only made her feel worse; it opened her up so she felt broken and jagged inside. She'd told him she'd wanted an amicable marriage, but now she wondered if Leo's coldness, even his snideness, would have been easier to handle. These little kindnesses hurt her, made her realise how much they'd both given up—and all because she hadn't felt strong or brave enough to risk the real thing.

But it was too late for regrets, she reminded herself as she took a piece of toast and munched obediently. And it was better this way. If she kept telling herself that perhaps she'd start to believe it.

Leo watched as Margo ate a piece of toast, her shoulders hunched against the winter wind, her face pale and composed now, although he could still see the sheen of tears in her dark eyes, turning them luminous and twisting his gut.

He didn't want her to cry. He had been angry and alarmed when he'd thought the doctor had hurt her during the ultrasound. He felt worse now, seeing her near tears. He still had feelings for Margo—feelings he had neither expected nor wanted to have. *Feelings which had led him to agreeing to this marriage.*

For the last four months he'd refused even to think of her. She'd been as good as dead to him. And since she'd come back into his life twenty-four hours ago he'd made sure to keep both his distance and his composure. But he hadn't been keeping either. He saw that now. He'd been fooling himself—punishing her with snide or sarcastic comments because it was easier than grabbing her by the shoulders and demanding to know why she'd left him. Or maybe just kissing her senseless.

Who cared what her reasons had been? She was here now.

And she rejected you once. Why shouldn't she again?

But he didn't need to punish her any more. Perhaps he never should have, if she really was telling the truth when she said there hadn't been anyone else. He could at least be amicable. Amicable and no more.

'We should get back,' he said. 'You look like you need a rest. And I need to arrange the wedding details.'

Margo's step faltered. 'The wedding? Already?'

'We'll marry tomorrow afternoon in a civil service here in Athens. Pending the paternity results, of course.' Margo looked dazed by that news, but he continued, an edge to his voice. 'Surely, considering our circumstances, you don't expect the whole church and white dress affair?'

Fire flashed in her eyes. 'Are you *really* so old-fashioned and chauvinistic?'

'How is that *either* of those things?' Leo demanded. 'We're getting married for the sake of this child, Margo—not because we love each other or even want to be with each other.'

He was saying it for his own sake as well as hers, and somehow that just made him even more furious. 'A church wedding would be a mockery.'

'And a white dress would too, I suppose?'

'This isn't some criticism of you,' Leo answered. 'It's simply a statement of fact and what our marriage really is. What it will be.'

'Fine,' Margo answered, her eyes still flashing. 'Fine,' she said again and, dropping the remnants of her toast in the bin, she walked past him towards the car.

CHAPTER SIX

SHE COULDN'T SLEEP. Margo had tossed and turned in the guest bedroom for several hours before she'd finally given up trying. It wasn't the bed—it was one of the most comfortable she'd ever slept in. And it wasn't that she wasn't tired, because she still felt exhausted. Even so her mind seethed with half-formed questions and thoughts, and they spun around in her brain until she decided to make herself some herbal tea in an attempt to help her sleep.

She reached for her dressing gown and the box of ginger tea she'd brought with her; it was one of the few things she could stomach. Tiptoeing out of her bedroom, not wanting to disturb Leo, she made her way to the kitchen.

The rest of the day had passed uneventfully enough: she'd had a nap and a bath while Leo had worked in his study. And at around dinnertime he'd knocked on her door and told her he was planning to order food in, asked her what she'd like.

It had reminded Margo painfully of the weekends they'd spent together in this hotel or that, drinking champagne and eating takeaway, making love. Weekends stolen from reality, and yet so precious to her. Weekends when she'd felt carefree and alive in a way she never had before—or since.

She'd thought those weekends had kept her safe, kept

her from being emotionally engaged. Emotionally vulnerable.

Now she knew she'd been a fool. And she was still being a fool, because every moment she spent with Leo made her feel more raw. More afraid.

The meal they'd shared tonight had been utterly different from those earlier ones. They'd sat at either end of a huge dining room table, a modern-looking thing of carved ebony, and Margo had picked at her plain pasta while Leo had eaten souvlaki and answered emails on his smartphone. Neither of them had spoken.

This, then, was her future. Silent meals and endless tension.

Would it have been different if she'd said yes to Leo's proposal? Or would they have ended up here anyway, because they'd never loved each other? At least, Leo hadn't loved *her.* And what she'd felt for Leo had been only the beginnings of something, a tender shoot that had been plucked from the barren soil of her heart before it could take root and grow.

She hadn't let herself truly love Leo because loving someone meant opening yourself up to pain, heartache and loss. She'd learned long ago that people left you. Her mother, her foster parents, her sister. *Oh, God, her sister.*

Margo closed her eyes and willed back the rush of memory and pain.

Leo wouldn't leave her. He had too much honour for that. And as for this child… She pressed a hand to her middle and closed her eyes. *Stay safe, little one*, she prayed silently. *Stay strong.*

She made a cup of ginger tea, cradling the warm mug in her hands, and curled up on a window seat in the living room. The huge bay window overlooked Kolonaki's wide boulevards and narrow side streets, now illuminated only by a few streetlights and a thin crescent moon high above. In the distance she could see the Acropolis, its ancient buildings lit at night, a beacon for the city.

She took a sip of tea and tried to settle her swirling thoughts, but they were like leaves in a storm and the moment she tried to snatch at one another blew away. She closed her eyes and leaned against the window frame, tried instead to think of nothing at all.

'Is everything all right?'

Margo opened her eyes to see Leo standing in the doorway, dressed only in a pair of navy silk pyjama bottoms that rested low on his trim hips. The sight of his bare chest, all sleek rippled muscle, the sprinkling of dark hair veeing down to the waistband of his pyjamas, made her heart lurch and the breath stop in her lungs. She knew how hot and satiny his skin could be. She remembered the feel of that crisp hair against her seeking fingers. She knew the intimate feel of his whole body pressed against hers, chest to breasts, hips bumping, legs tangled.

She stared at him, willing herself to speak, not to want. 'I couldn't sleep,' she finally managed, her voice coming out in little more than a croak. 'I made some tea to help me settle. I'm sorry if I disturbed you.'

'I couldn't sleep either,' he said, and to her shock he came to sit down beside her on the window seat, his hip nudging her toes. 'Why couldn't you sleep?' he asked quietly.

'Why couldn't *you*?' Answering his question with one of her own was easier than admitting all the fears and worries that were tumbling through her mind.

'It's a lot to process,' Leo said after a moment. 'A baby, marriage… Just over twenty-four hours ago I wasn't anticipating either.'

'No, I suppose I've had more time to deal with it.'

He glanced down at her bare feet and then wrapped one warm hand around her foot. Everything in Margo jolted hard, almost painfully, at the feel of his strong hand curled around the sensitive arch of her foot, his fingers touching her toes.

'Your feet are cold,' he said, and drew them towards him, tucking them under his leg just as he had so many times before, when they'd been together.

Margo simply sat there, rigid with shock, with both of her feet tucked under his legs, everything in her aching.

'When you found out you were pregnant…' Leo asked slowly. 'How did it happen? How did you feel?'

Margo tensed, wondering if this was some kind of trap. Was he attempting to remind her once again of how non-maternal she'd been? Because she knew that. Of course she knew that, and it fed her fear.

'Why do you ask?'

'I just want to know. I feel like I've missed a big part of this.'

'I'm only four months along, Leo,' Margo said, but she relaxed slightly because she believed him. This wasn't a trap. Not with the sincerity she heard in his voice and her feet tucked under his legs.

'I had no idea at the start,' she began. 'I was on the pill, as you know. I didn't even miss taking one.'

'Then how did you get pregnant?'

'The day after…' She swallowed, felt a blush heat her cheeks and hoped Leo couldn't see in the dark. 'The day after I saw you I slept in. I took the pill three hours later than I normally would.'

'And that was enough to keep it from working?'

With a self-conscious laugh she patted her little bump. 'Apparently the mini-pill has to be taken at exactly the same time every day—although I didn't know things were quite that strict until it was too late.'

'You must have been shocked.'

'I was in a complete daze. I…I didn't know what I was going to do.' She hesitated in making that admission, afraid that Leo would use it against her, but he just nodded.

'That's understandable.'

'So for a while I didn't do anything. And then I felt so sick I *couldn't* do anything but drag myself through each day. When I went to the doctor to get some medication for my nausea he said something—just a throwaway comment about how such sickness usually meant the baby was healthy. "Here to stay," is what he said. And I knew that he was speaking the truth. That this baby was here to stay…that my inertia had been out of—well, out of fear,' she said.

Suddenly she realised just how much she was revealing. But she hadn't talked about this to anyone, and it felt good to unburden herself a little. Or even a lot.

'Fear?' Leo frowned. 'What are you afraid of?'

So many things. 'Of what the future would look like,' Margo answered, knowing she was hedging. 'Of how it would work. And of how you would take the news—what it would mean.'

'And so you decided to ask me to marry you?' Leo said. 'I still don't understand *that*, Margo.'

She swallowed, her throat feeling tight and sore. 'I grew up without a father,' she said after a brief pause. 'I didn't want the same for my child.'

He was silent for a moment. Then, 'I don't actually know anything about your childhood.'

And there was a very good reason for that. 'We didn't share many confidences, really, during our…' She trailed off.

'Our fling?' Leo filled in tonelessly.

'Yes.'

Even though her toes were still tucked under his warm thigh she felt a coolness in the air, tension tauten between them. It was a timely reminder of just what they'd had together...and what they had now.

'You want this baby,' Leo said slowly, a statement.

He lifted his head to look her straight in the face, and even in the darkness she could see the serious, intent look on his face, although she didn't know what it meant.

'Yes, I do.'

'You've changed in that, then?'

She took a deep breath and nodded. 'Yes.'

'Why?'

She stared at him, knowing he deserved to know at least this much. 'I didn't want children before because I was afraid,' she said slowly. 'Afraid of loving someone...and losing them. Or of getting it wrong. Parenting is a huge responsibility, Leo. The biggest.'

'But one you feel ready to take on now?'

'With your help.'

Except she didn't feel ready, not remotely. She felt inadequate and afraid and guilty. Because she wasn't sure she deserved another chance with someone's life.

'I *will* help you, Margo,' Leo said. 'We can do this. Together.'

She smiled even as she blinked back tears. She wanted to believe him. She almost did.

'I hope the tea helps you sleep,' he said, nodding towards her cup.

Margo knew he was about to leave and realised she didn't want him to.

'Leo...thank you,' she said, her voice both hurried and soft.

He stopped and turned to look at her in surprise. 'What are you thanking me for?'

'For...for being kind.'

He let out a huff of sound—almost a laugh. 'I don't think I've actually been very kind to you, Margo.'

'I know you were angry. I know you thought I'd cheated on you—maybe you still do. But even so you've agreed to marry me, and you've—you've shown concern for my welfare. I do appreciate that.'

He gazed at her for a long, fathomless moment before rising from the window seat. 'That's not very much, really.'

'I'm still grateful.'

It seemed as if he were going to say something else, something important, and Margo caught her breath... waited.

But all he said was, 'Get some sleep,' before returning to the darkness of his bedroom.

Leo stretched out on his bed and stared up at the ceiling, as far from sleep as he'd ever been. So much had happened today, tender little moments that had left him feeling uneasy and raw. It would be easy, he realised, to let himself care about Margo again. Let himself fall in love with her.

Let himself be rejected. Again.

Whatever had kept Margo from being with him before, it was still there. He didn't know what it was—the conversation he'd just had with her had left him wondering, uncertain. He'd seen a new vulnerability and fear underneath Margo's glossy, confident sophistication, and it had shocked him. It had made him realise there was depth and sadness to the woman with whom he'd had a passionate affair. The woman he was going to marry tomorrow.

The results of the paternity test were nothing more than a formality; he knew the baby was his. He knew Margo knew it. And with a baby and a marriage they could, in time, begin to build something together. Maybe not a grand passion or love, but something good and real and strong.

Then he reminded himself with slamming force of how she'd refused to marry him just four months ago, when they'd still been having their *fling*. She still clearly viewed their marriage as a sacrifice. How could he build on *that*—and, even if he could, why would he want to?

He'd had enough of trying to win people's trust or affection. For his entire childhood he'd been desperate for his father to notice him, love him. But Evangelos Marakaios had only cared about his business, and about handing it to his oldest son. In his mind Leo had been nothing more than spare—unneeded, irrelevant.

When his father had died Leo had hoped that his older brother Antonios would include him more in the family business, that they would have a partnership. But Antonios had cut him off even more than his father had, making him nothing more than a frontman, the eye candy to bring in new business without actually having any serious responsibility.

All that had changed six months ago, when Antonios had finally told Leo the truth. Evangelos had been borrowing against the company, making shoddy and sometimes illegal investments and running everything into debt. He'd hidden it from everyone except Antonios, confessing all when he'd been on his deathbed. Antonios had spent the next ten years hiding it from Leo.

He'd finally told the truth when prompted by his wife Lindsay and by Leo's own furious demands. And, while Leo had been glad to finally learn the truth, the knowledge didn't erase ten years of hurt, of anger, of being intentionally misled. His father and his brother, two of the people most important to him, had lied to him. They hadn't trusted him, and nothing they'd done had made Leo believe they loved him.

After so many years of trying to make them do both, he was far from eager to try the same with his soon-to-be wife.

He let out a weary sigh and closed his eyes, willed sleep to come. Enough thinking about Margo and what might have been. All he could do was take one day at a time and guard his heart. Make this marriage what they'd both agreed it would be: businesslike and convenient, and, yes, amicable. But nothing more.

Never anything more.

CHAPTER SEVEN

IF BRIDES WERE meant to look radiant on their wedding day, Margo thought, she fell lamentably short. She still had the exhausted, washed-out look she'd been sporting since the nausea had first hit, and she was, according to Leo's plan, going to get married this afternoon.

Sighing, she dragged a brush through her dark hair and wondered which of the two outfits she'd brought would be better to get married in—a sweater dress or jeans?

She didn't actually want the whole white wedding affair that Leo had mocked yesterday, but even so it felt pathetic and sad to be married like this, in the clothes she'd travelled in, looking like death barely warmed over.

With a sigh, she pulled her hair back into a neat ponytail and went in search of Leo.

She found him in the dining alcove of the kitchen, where the wide windows overlooked the small garden at the back of the townhouse. He'd made breakfast: toast and coffee, yogurt and fruit.

'I know you probably can't manage anything,' he said, gesturing to all the food, 'but I thought I'd make it just in case.'

'Thank you,' Margo murmured and sat down.

She spooned a little fruit and yogurt into a bowl and stirred honey into the centre.

Leo rose from the table and a few seconds later brought back a mug of ginger tea.

Margo blinked in surprise. 'How—?'

'You left the box of sachets in the kitchen. It seems like something you can keep down.'

'Just about the only thing.'

'Don't forget melba toast.'

'Right.'

She took a sip of tea and tried to still her swirling thoughts. Leo's consideration made her feel both restless and uneasy. It would have been easier to deal with his businesslike briskness, even his coldness, but this kindness… it reached right inside her. It made her ache with both regret and longing.

'Why are you doing this, Leo?' she asked.

'Doing what?'

'This.' She gestured to the breakfast dishes. 'You're being so…considerate.'

He gave her the ghost of a smile. 'Is that a bad thing?'

'No, but…'

'I don't want to fight all the time, Margo. That's not good for either of us, or our child.' He hesitated and then said, 'The doctor's office called this morning with the results of the paternity test.'

So that was the reason for his kindness and consideration. 'So now you know.'

'And you knew all along.'

'I told you there wasn't anyone else, Leo.'

'I believe you.'

He didn't look particularly pleased, though, and Margo wondered if the truth had hurt him as much as her lie had. Could he ever understand the desperate fear that had driven her to act as she had? She didn't even want him to.

'The marriage ceremony is at the town hall, at two

o'clock,' he said after a pause. 'We can drive back to the estate afterwards.'

'All right.'

'We need two witnesses for the ceremony,' he continued. 'I thought I'd ask two of my staff from the Athens office.'

'Fine.'

It wasn't the way she'd ever anticipated getting married —a cold ceremony in a bureaucrat's office in a country she didn't know—but then she'd never anticipated marrying at all. She'd expected to live her life alone, the way she had since she was twelve and she'd lost everyone. *She'd lost Annelise.*

Leo glanced at the rumpled sweater dress she'd worn two days in a row. 'Do you have something to wear to the wedding?'

'I wasn't planning to get married today,' she reminded him. 'I have this or jeans.'

He frowned and took a sip of coffee. 'Then we'll go shopping this morning for something suitable. If you feel up to it?'

She almost asked him why they should bother, but then just nodded instead. Leo had said arguing would be unpleasant for both of them, and she agreed. She would do her part in keeping things civil, even if his kindness had a strange way of hurting her.

Half an hour later they were strolling down Voukourestiou Street, home to many designer boutiques. Leo led her into the first one, a soaring space of airy lightness, with a white leather sofa where shoppers could rest and a few select garments hanging from silver wires suspended from the ceiling.

Margo glanced at the elegant gowns in bemusement, for she had no idea what kind of dress she was supposed to get married in. But this was a business arrangement, so a business outfit seemed appropriate. She saw a pale grey suit at the back of the boutique and nodded to it.

'How about that one?'

Leo frowned. 'That doesn't look much like a wedding dress.'

'This isn't much of a wedding,' she answered.

His frown deepened. 'We might be marrying in a civil ceremony, but it is still very much a wedding. We will still very much be married.'

He nodded towards a dress of cream silk with an empire waist and a frothy skirt glittering with beaded crystals.

'How about that one?'

It was a feminine, frou-frou kind of dress—so unlike her usual tailored wardrobe. Margo hesitated, because while it wasn't something she would normally wear, she *did* like it. It was different. It wasn't armour.

She gave a quick nod. 'All right. I'll try it on.'

Moments later she stared at herself in the mirror, surprised at how the dress softened her. The warm cream of the material actually brought a bit of colour to her face, and complemented her dark hair and eyes. The sales assistant had brought her a matching pair of shoes—slim heels with a small diamante on each toe. They went perfectly with the dress.

'Well?' Leo called.

'You're not supposed to see it before the ceremony,' Margo called back. 'But I think it will do.'

At the cash desk she offered to pay for it, but Leo silenced her with a single look as he handed over his credit card. He'd been the same when they were dating: he'd paid for all their meals and hotels, despite Margo's insistence that she could pay her way. She hadn't minded, because she'd still felt safe. Still kept him at a distance.

This felt different. This was a wedding dress—the start of a new life that would be utterly intertwined with Leo's.

'We should go back to the apartment,' he said as he accepted the dress, now swathed in a designer hanging bag. 'You should rest before the ceremony.'

A few hours later Margo's stomach was seething with a whole different kind of nausea, now caused by nervousness. She'd showered and put on her new dress and heels, coiled her hair into its usual elegant chignon. The dress's high waist hid her small baby bump, for which she was grateful. She'd rather not have some sanctimonious city official looking at her disapprovingly.

'Are you ready?' Leo called, and she gave her reflection one last, swift look.

In less than an hour she would be married. She would have made vows that would bind her to Leo for ever.

'I'm coming,' she called, and walked out of the bedroom.

Leo's eyes widened as he took in her appearance, and then he gave one nod. 'You look very nice.'

It was a rather 'milquetoast' compliment, but Margo saw the way colour touched his cheekbones. She felt awareness—physical awareness—sweep through her in an electrifying wave.

'You look nice too,' she said, which was a serious understatement.

In a dark grey suit and silvery-grey tie he looked amazing. The colour of his tie made his eyes look even more silver, seeming to blaze in his swarthy face, and his dark hair was brushed back, the strong lines of his cheekbones and jaw emphasised by the cut of his suit.

'We should drive to the town hall,' he said. 'And then

we can leave directly from there. I need to get back to the estate to work.'

Margo nodded. No matter how incredible Leo looked, this marriage was still no more than a business arrangement. 'I'll get my bag.'

They drove in silence to the town hall, with tension stretching and snapping between them, or at least that was how it felt to Margo. She knew the civil marriage ceremony would be short and simple, but she would still be making promises to Leo. To herself. To their baby. Promises she intended to keep. Which made her heart race and her hands go clammy. There would be no going back from this.

The town hall in Athens was an impressive building in the centre of the city; the marriage ceremony was to be held in a small room on a top floor, with only a few people in attendance. The two staff from Leo's office greeted him with bland faces, although Margo imagined they had to be curious as to why their CEO was getting married in such a quick and pragmatic way. Thank goodness her bump wasn't visible, although of course it would be soon enough.

The official cleared his throat and began, and within a few minutes it was over. Margo had barely had to say a word.

Leo slid a ring of white gold on her finger; she stared down at it in surprise.

'When did you...?'

'I had it couriered,' he answered, and for some reason it hurt her—the thought that someone else had bought her wedding ring.

It was stupid, of course, but then she'd been so emotional lately. In any case, Margo knew she'd have to get used to these little things and remind herself that they weren't slights. She hadn't wanted romance, so she shouldn't expect it. Its absence surely shouldn't hurt her.

Just like the fact that he hadn't kissed her shouldn't hurt. It was simply the way it was. And so they walked out of the town hall into the bright winter sunshine, and then to the car.

They drove out of Athens as husband and wife, with not one word or person to mark the occasion.

Leo drove in silence for nearly an hour, his mind seething with thoughts he didn't want to articulate. The ceremony had been both simple and brief, which was how he'd expected and wanted it to be, and yet somehow he felt as if he were disappointing Margo. Disappointing himself.

It had hardly seemed appropriate to have a big church wedding, and yet… It had been a very small ceremony for a big step such as they were taking.

He glanced at the ring she'd slid onto his finger, her fingers seeming so fragile and cold on his. *Married.* He was a husband now, with responsibilities to his wife and child. Responsibilities he'd bear gladly, and yet he still felt their weight.

And one of those responsibilities was introducing Margo to his family. He hadn't considered the ramifications of marrying quickly and bringing Margo back to his villa immediately after. He'd simply wanted to control the situation, to have it on his terms.

Now he realised two of his sisters, Xanthe and Ava, who lived on the estate with him, would be wide-eyed and speculating when he brought back his sudden and obviously pregnant bride.

His older brother Antonios had done virtually the same thing—coming back from a business trip to North America with his unexpected bride, Lindsay. Antonios's iron will had assured Lindsay was made welcome, but even so Leo had seen how hard it had been on her, for a variety of reasons. And she hadn't even been pregnant.

He didn't want the same rocky start for Margo.

Flexing his hands on the steering wheel, he glanced at her, looking so pale and weary. 'My sisters will be at the estate when we return,' he began, and she turned to him sharply.

'Sisters? I didn't even know you *had* sisters.'

'Three, and one brother.'

'Your brother I know about. He was CEO before you?'

'Yes.' He'd told her that much at least, although he hadn't even hinted at the strains and sins that had marred their relationship. 'Two of my sisters live on the estate. They will want to meet you.'

'They weren't there before when I came?'

'No, they were visiting Parthenope, my third sister. She lives with her family near Patras.'

'Timon's mother?'

'Yes.'

Margo expelled a shaky breath. 'And what about your parents?'

'They're both dead.'

'I'm sorry.' She glanced at him, her eyes dark. 'When?'

'My father ten years ago, and my mother six months ago.'

Her eyes widened. 'When we were together?'

'Yes.'

He hadn't told her. There was so much he hadn't told her. And for the first time Leo acknowledged how Margo had had a point, claiming their relationship hadn't been going anywhere. He'd kept inside its careful parameters as much as she had. It was only when he'd become CEO that he'd decided he should marry and have an heir, and Margo had seemed the obvious choice. The right choice.

And now it had all happened just as he'd wanted…and yet not at all as he'd expected.

'They won't be pleased, will they?' Margo said after a moment. 'To welcome a surprise sister-in-law, and one who's pregnant?'

'They'll be surprised,' Leo allowed.

Margo let out a huff of laughter. 'I should say so. Did they even know you were—that we were—?'

'No.' He shifted in his seat. 'I never told anyone about us.'

She eyed him curiously. 'And yet you asked me to marry you?'

'I know.' He hesitated, and then continued a bit stiffly, 'I realise now how surprising my proposal must have been. Regardless of how you felt about it, it had to have been a shock.'

'It was.' She took a breath. 'Why…why did you ask me, Leo? If you didn't love me?'

'It felt like the right time to get married. I'd just been made CEO and I was conscious of needing an heir, stability. And as we were already together…'

'It was convenient?'

She let out another huff of sound, although whether it was a laugh or something else Leo couldn't tell.

'Well, that's what it is now. *Convenient.*'

'In any case,' Leo continued, 'I want to make sure my family accepts you as mistress of the household. You'll have my full support—'

'I don't want to displace anyone.'

'As my wife, you will have a role—'

'I know.' She leaned her head back against the seat and closed her eyes. 'I know. And I will rise to that particular challenge, I promise you. Just…just give me some time—please?'

'What about *your* family?' he asked, deciding it was wiser, or at least safer, to leave the topic of his own family for now. 'Is there anyone you want to tell? You could invite them to come—'

'No,' she cut across him flatly, her face turned to the window. 'There's no one.'

'Your parents?' Belatedly he remembered she'd said she'd grown up without a father. 'Your mother, at least?'

'I haven't seen her since I was twelve.'

'Really?'

Perhaps he shouldn't have been shocked. In the last few days he'd sensed a sorrow, even a darkness, in Margo's past that he'd never noticed before, perhaps because she'd been careful to hide it.

'Why not?'

She twitched her shoulders in a shrug. 'She wasn't a very good mother.'

It was clear she didn't want to talk about it, and Leo decided not to press. There had been enough emotional upheavals today.

'I'm sorry,' he said, and she bowed her head, a few tendrils of hair escaping her ponytail to rest against her cheek.

'So am I,' she said, and she sounded so sad that Leo felt an answering emotion rise in him in an unstoppable tide.

For a moment he considered pulling the car over, pulling her into his arms. Making her feel better.

But then she raised her head, set her jaw, and that moment passed almost as if it had never happened at all.

They didn't speak until they reached Amfissa.

CHAPTER EIGHT

MARGO FORCED HERSELF to relax as Leo turned the car up the sweeping drive that led to the Marakaios estate. She'd seen it all before, of course, when she'd driven up here in her rental car just two days ago. But then it had just been a house, grand and imposing; now it was her home.

As he pulled the car up to the front of the sprawling villa she noticed the other buildings surrounding it. The Marakaios estate was actually a complex, almost a little city.

'What are all the other buildings?'

'The office, a guesthouse, staff housing, a private villa where I used to live before I moved to the main house.'

'When was that?'

'When I became CEO.'

Which seemed to have been a life-changing moment, with his moving and then thinking of marrying.

'Why did your brother step down?'

'He wanted to move into investments,' Leo said, and the terseness of his reply made Margo wonder if there were more to it than that. She really knew so little about this man, her *husband*. So little about his life, his family.

And some of his family were coming out of the house right now: two tall, dark-haired women with the same striking good looks as Leo. Margo was intimidated by them already, and they hadn't even seen her yet, or her bump.

As Leo climbed out of the car the first one addressed him in a torrent of Greek, her hands on her hips. Distantly Margo considered that perhaps she should learn her husband's native language. Lessons, at least, would fill her empty days until the baby was born.

Leo came round to open the passenger door as his other sister joined them, unleashing her own incomprehensible diatribe. Leo didn't answer, just extended a hand to Margo.

She rose from the seat, still in her wedding dress, and as she stood the material caught on the door and tugged tight, outlining her small bump. Both sisters stopped abruptly and sucked in their breaths.

'*Kalispera,*' Margo said, and pinned on a bright and utterly false smile.

One of the sisters turned to Leo and began speaking again in rapid Greek. He held up a hand to silence her. 'Speak English, please, Xanthe. You're perfectly capable of it. My wife does not speak Greek.'

'Your *wife*—' Xanthe said, and her mouth dropped open.

She looked, Margo thought, appalled.

'Yes. My wife. We married today and, as you can see, we are expecting our first child in a few months.' He placed a hand on Margo's lower back, propelling her forward. 'Xanthe, Ava—please meet Margo Ferrars, Margo Marakaios now.'

She smiled weakly.

'Margo—my sisters.'

'I'm pleased to meet you,' she said, and they both nodded stiffly. Margo couldn't really blame them for the lack of welcome; they were clearly completely shocked. Still, it stung.

'Come inside,' Leo said, and drew her past his sisters into the villa.

Maria bustled up to them as soon as they stepped inside the door, and Leo spoke to her in Greek before turning to Margo with a grimace of apology. 'Maria doesn't speak English, but I've told her we're married.'

Margo nodded. She couldn't tell a thing from the housekeeper's expression, but she felt too overwhelmed and exhausted to care. It had been an incredibly long day, and she didn't have the energy to deal with any of these strangers.

'Leo,' she said, 'I'm tired, and I'd like to rest.'

It was only a little past seven, yet even so Margo knew she couldn't face an evening with Leo's family. Was she neglecting her responsibilities, even her vows, so soon? So be it. Tomorrow she would try to be the Stepford Wife he seemed to want. Today she needed to recover.

'Of course. I'll show you to your bedroom.'

Margo felt the silent stares boring into her back as she followed Leo up to the bedrooms. He went down a different corridor than before, and then ushered her into a sumptuous room decorated in pale blue and ivory.

'This is your bedroom. I have an adjoining one.' He gestured to a wood-panelled door in the corner, by the window.

So they wouldn't be sharing a bedroom. Margo didn't know how she felt about that, and in her exhausted state didn't feel like probing the tangle of her own emotions.

'Thank you,' she murmured, and took a few steps into the bedroom.

'You must let Maria know if you would like anything,' Leo said. 'And I'll be right next door if you need something in the night…'

She swallowed painfully. A lump had risen in her throat and it was hard to speak around it. It was their wedding night and they would be sleeping apart. She knew she shouldn't expect, much less want anything else.

'I'll be fine,' she said, and he nodded, one hand on the doorknob, seeming reluctant to leave her.

But he did, and Margo sank onto the bed and dropped her head into her hands. She felt more alone, more isolated, than she had in a long, long while—and considering the lonely course of her life, the loss of both her mother and Annelise, that was saying something.

She missed her apartment desperately, with its cosy, familiar furnishings, its sense of safety. She missed her life, the job that had given her security and purpose, her friends like Sophie, who might not have known that much about her but had still been *friends.*

She should text Sophie and tell her everything that had happened... But Margo didn't think she had it in her to weather Sophie's undoubtedly stunned and concerned response. No, she'd sleep. And maybe in the morning it would all look a little bit better.

At least their wedding night, wretched as it was, would be over.

Leo sat alone in his bedroom and stared moodily out of the window. He'd endured a barrage of questions from his sisters, who had wanted to know how he'd met Margo and why he'd married her.

'You might have noticed she's carrying my child,' he'd said tersely.

Xanthe had rolled her eyes. 'It's the twenty-first century, Leo. Illegitimacy isn't the stigma it once was.'

'I'm a traditional man.'

But he hadn't simply married Margo because she was pregnant with his baby, he acknowledged now. That might have been the impetus, but the truth was he'd wanted to marry her. He'd wanted her four months ago and he wanted her now.

And now it was his wedding night, and he was sitting here alone, drinking his second whisky, when what he really wanted was to take Margo into his arms and feel her softness against him…

Muttering a curse, Leo finished his whisky in one burning swallow. It was going to be a long, long night.

When Margo woke up the next morning she felt a lump of dread in her middle, as heavy as a stone, at the thought of facing the day and Leo's sisters, his staff…facing this whole strange world that she was now a part of.

She lay in bed and blinked up at the ceiling as wintry sunlight filtered through the curtains and illuminated the room's luxurious furnishings. For a girl who had been a breath away from growing up on the streets, she really had landed in a soft place indeed.

Resolutely Margo swung her legs over the side of the bed. After the usual moment of dizziness passed, she rose. She might not be looking forward to today, but she would meet it. She'd certainly faced far worse. And no matter how uncertain of her or unfriendly Leo's sisters might be, this was her new life. She had to accept it. Embrace it, even.

With that in mind, Margo put on her last remaining outfit, jeans and a jumper, and headed downstairs.

She could hear Leo's sisters' voices from the dining room as she came downstairs. They spoke in Greek, but Margo didn't need to know the language to understand the gist of what they were saying. Agitation, hurt and anger were audible in their tones.

She took a deep breath, squared her shoulders, and entered the room. '*Kalimera*.' Her knowledge of Greek extended only to greetings and saying thank you, but she hoped she was at least showing them she was trying.

Xanthe and Ava fell silent, forcing smiles to their lips. Margo sat at the opposite end of the table from Leo and busied herself with putting a napkin on her lap. She could see yogurt, fresh fruit and pastries on the table, and coffee, tea and juice on the sideboard. She wasn't very hungry but, wanting something to do, began to fill her plate.

'Good morning,' Leo answered her in English, and from the corner of her eye Margo saw him give a pointed look to his sisters. 'Did you sleep well?'

Margo felt a ripple of surprise from his sisters, and knew they were wondering why Leo should ask such a question. It would soon be clear to everyone that they had not shared a bedroom.

Leo must have realised it too, for his mouth tightened and he took a sip of coffee.

'I slept very well, thank you,' Margo said quietly.

They sounded like polite strangers. His sisters' eyes were on stalks.

'I thought perhaps after breakfast I could show you around the estate a bit,' Leo continued, his tone stiff now with formality. 'If you feel up to it?'

'That would be good.'

They sounded as if they were ironing out the details of a business merger—which was, Margo supposed, essentially what they were doing. If Leo wanted their marriage to be businesslike, then she supposed he wouldn't mind his sisters knowing it.

'Leo hasn't told us anything about you,' Xanthe said after a few moments of strained silence, when all Margo did was toy with her food and stare at her plate. 'Where are you from?'

She looked up and met Xanthe's speculative gaze with what she hoped was a friendly smile. 'I lived in Paris.'

'I love Paris!'

Ava jumped in quickly, and Margo wondered if the sisters would actually be welcoming towards her after all.

'It must have been very hard to leave.'

Margo glanced at Leo, whose face was as bland as ever. 'A bit,' she allowed, 'but I have other things to think about now.'

She rested one hand on her small bump, which unintentionally but effectively silenced all conversation. Both Xanthe and Ava excused themselves a few minutes later, leaving Leo and Margo alone with about an acre of polished mahogany between them.

'I'm sorry things seem a bit awkward,' Leo said after a moment. 'They'll come to accept you in time.'

'Maybe,' Margo allowed. 'I don't suppose it really matters.'

'Doesn't it? This is your home now, Margo. My family is your family. I want you to feel a part of things. I want you to *be* a part of things.'

'I know.' She toyed with a piece of melon and then laid down her fork. 'I'll hold up my end of the bargain, Leo.'

To her surprise he threw his napkin down and rose from the table. 'I don't want to talk about bargains,' he said. 'Let me know when you are ready to begin the tour. I'll be in my study.'

Mystified, Margo watched him stride out of the dining room. She'd annoyed him, obviously, but she didn't know how or why. Sighing, feeling the day stretching out in front of her would be very long indeed, she ate a bit of yogurt and nibbled on a pastry before rising herself and going to find Leo.

He'd told her he would be in the study, but she couldn't remember where it was—although she certainly recalled the interview she'd had in there just two days ago. She pressed a hand to her forehead, amazed at how much had changed in such a short time. Her whole life had been up-ended.

After opening and closing a few doors that led to various impressive reception rooms, she finally found the study. Leo sat behind the desk, one hand driving through his hair, rumpling it in a way that would have made him seem endearing if he hadn't had such a scowl on his face.

Margo knocked on the already open door and Leo looked up. His face cleared, but only just.

'Did you eat something?'

'A bit. I'm fine.'

He hesitated, then said, 'Things will get better. As you settle in.'

'I hope so. Although I'm not sure what you want sometimes, Leo. You almost seemed angry back there, talking about our marriage as a bargain, and yet *you're* the one who said you wanted to keep it businesslike.' The words spilled out of her, even though she hadn't intended to say them.

'I know,' Leo said, and drummed his fingers on the desktop.

Margo waited for him to elaborate but he didn't.

'I just want us to be on the same page,' she said quietly. 'Whatever page that is.'

'I think it will take time to decide what page that is,' he said finally. 'But in the meantime we can deal with practical matters.' He nodded towards her jeans and jumper. 'You need clothes and toiletries. We can order some things online, or go into Amfissa—'

'I'd like to get my things from Paris,' Margo answered. 'I'll need to speak to people at work, put my apartment on the market.'

'There's no need to sell your apartment. I can certainly afford to keep it, and it might be nice for us to have a permanent place in Paris.'

She blinked, surprised by his generosity. It was a far cry from the conditions he'd given her the last time they'd been in this room. 'Are you—are you sure?'

'Yes. Why shouldn't we keep it?' He stared at her for a moment and then said, his voice gaining an edge, 'Not *everything* about our marriage has to be a sacrifice, Margo.'

'I didn't mean it like that—'

'No? Sometimes when you look at me you seem as if you're steeling yourself.' He rose from the desk, shrugging on his suit jacket. 'It seems strange that it is so difficult for you to spend time with me now when we had two years together. But perhaps when you said you were planning to end it you spoke the truth, whether there was another man or not.'

He spoke with such bland indifference that it took Margo a few seconds for his meaning to penetrate. 'Leo, I thought it was you who didn't want to spend time with *me*. You've been angry with me for months, and I understand why—'

'I'm not angry.'

'No? If I look like I'm steeling myself,' Margo said, her heart starting to beat hard at this sudden, unexpected honesty, 'it's because I'm bracing myself for whatever mood you're in—whatever you're going to say. Sometimes… sometimes it feels like you're still punishing me for leaving you.'

He stared at her for a long moment, his eyes like shards of ice in his fathomless face. Margo waited, her breath held.

'I'm not punishing you,' he said at last. 'Not any more. I admit when you first came here…when I believed you'd been unfaithful…I may have been acting out of anger, or even spite.' He sighed, the sound weary. 'A petty, useless emotion if ever there was one. But I don't want to act like that any more. We need to move on, Margo, and make this marriage something we can both live with.'

'Which is?'

'That I don't know yet. But hopefully we'll find out in time.' He moved past her towards the door. 'Now, let me show you the rest of the villa.'

She followed him through the house as he showed her various rooms: a formal living room and a smaller, cosier TV room, the large dining room where they'd had breakfast, and another less formal room for family meals. A music room, a library, a second kitchen for parties... Margo started to feel overwhelmed. The house was huge. And Leo wanted *her* to be its mistress.

'What exactly do you want me to do, Leo?' she asked as they left the second kitchen.

He turned to her with a frown. 'What do you mean?'

'I mean what are my responsibilities? You mentioned that you wanted me to be in charge of your household...'

'I only meant that as a courtesy to you and your position here. I don't expect you to have *duties*.'

Which made her feel more confused than ever. 'I don't understand...'

'Margo, we're married. You're the—'

'Mistress of the house? The chatelaine? Yes, I understand that.'

'You can do as much or as little as you like. If you want to consult with Maria about meals, or housekeeping, or anything, you're more than welcome. If you want to redecorate, go ahead. I'm trying to give you freedom, not a burden.'

'Thank you,' Margo said after a moment, because she didn't know what else to say.

She might have established her career in acquiring household items for a large department store, but even so she wasn't about to bring her skills to bear here. She doubted his sisters would appreciate her changing so much as a cushion. As for meals… Her cooking skills had always been limited. She couldn't imagine planning meals for everyone.

And yet…

This was her life. She needed to own it.

'Do Xanthe and Ava both eat in the main house?' she asked. 'Will we have meals with them every day?'

'They come and go. Neither of them really work, although Xanthe does a little PR for Marakaios Enterprises. Ava travels to Athens frequently. I suspect she's seeing someone there, but she's quite close-mouthed on the subject.'

So she'd have both women underfoot…watching and judging her. Margo pressed a hand to her middle to suppress the lurch of queasiness that prospect gave her.

Leo, of course, noticed.

'Are you well?'

'I'm fine, Leo. I'm actually feeling a bit better today than yesterday.' A good night's sleep and no more travelling had helped in that regard. 'But I do need some more clothes and things.'

'I can take you into Amfissa this afternoon for some supplies. And, if you'd like to make a list, I'll arrange for whatever possessions you want to be sent here from your apartment in Paris.'

'All right,' Margo said. And although she didn't like the thought of some stranger rifling through her things she had the sense to know that another long trip would exhaust her, and she appreciated Leo's kindness.

He took her upstairs, where he pointed out Xanthe and Ava's bedrooms, in a separate wing from theirs. And then he hesitated before opening the door to a slightly smaller bedroom next to hers.

'I thought, when the times comes, this could be the nursery.'

She glanced at the beautiful yet bland room, decorated in pale greens and creams.

'You can completely redecorate it, of course. Have you…?' He cleared his throat. 'Have you given some thought as to whether you'd like to know if it's a boy or girl?'

Shock rippled through her at the question; it raised a host of images and possibilities in her mind. Pink frilled dresses or blue romper suits. And whatever this child was—boy or girl—*they* would be the parents. Together they'd be raising this person, putting this tiny being at the centre of their shared lives.

'I don't think I've let myself,' she said slowly.

'What do you mean?'

She swallowed, not wanting to admit how fearful she was, about so many things. How even now she was terrified of losing this child, of something going terribly wrong.

'So far I've just wanted to make sure the baby is healthy,' she said. 'Do *you* want to find out?'

'I haven't thought about it,' Leo answered, rubbing his jaw. 'But I think…yes. If you do. It could help us prepare. Make it more real.'

Again she thought of the swooshing sound of the baby's heartbeat, the reality of this life inside her, so small and vulnerable, so *important*. 'Yes, I suppose it would.'

'Dr Tallos has recommended a local obstetrician,' he said. 'You're meant to have an ultrasound in three weeks.'

'Just before Christmas.'

And what a wonderful Christmas present that would be—the promise of a healthy baby, boy or girl.

Something must have shown in her face, for Leo stopped to look at her seriously, and then took her chin in his hand, his touch light, his gaze searching.

'Margo, what is it?'

'What do you mean?'

'You seem…afraid.'

Her throat tightened and she tried to smile. 'I just don't want anything to go wrong with the baby.'

'Why do you think something might?'

Because she knew what it was like to lose someone precious. One day Annelise had been there—soft and smiling and warm, with her button-black eyes and her round cherubic cheeks—and the next she'd been gone. There had been nothing left but emptiness and heartbreak.

'Margo…' Leo said again, and he sounded alarmed.

She knew she must have an awful expression on her face.

She stepped back, away from his hand. 'I'm a first-time mother,' she reminded him as lightly as she could. 'I'm bound to be nervous.'

But judging by Leo's frown she didn't think she'd fooled him into believing that was all it was.

CHAPTER NINE

A WEEK PASSED and Margo started to think she and Leo were finding that same page. Things had settled, more or less, into a routine: Leo worked most of the day and Margo drifted. She didn't mind it for now, because with her nausea and her exhaustion drifting through each day was about all she could manage.

But as the days passed, and her nausea thankfully started to abate, she knew she needed to find some focus. Some purpose.

Xanthe and Ava had thawed towards her a little, which made life less tense if not exactly easy. And her things had arrived from Paris. Besides her clothes and toiletries she'd requested that some of her personal items—paintings and ornaments and books—be shipped to Greece. It felt both comforting and strange to arrange her things in the bedroom that still didn't feel like hers. They were dotted around the yawning space like buoys bobbing in an unfamiliar sea.

Still, life marched on, and Margo knew she needed to march with it.

She drove into Amfissa one afternoon and wandered the streets, window-shopping. She went into a shop that sold nursery furniture and gazed in wonder at the array of cradles and buggies—at a whole arsenal of parental tools with which *she* would one day need to be equipped.

When she came back down the sweeping drive that led to the main villa of the Marakaios estate Leo came out of the house, standing on the portico as he glowered at her.

She hadn't even cut the engine before he was striding over to the driver's side and opening door.

'Where were you—?'

'In Amfissa. I told Maria.' She'd managed to learn enough Greek, and Maria knew enough English, to communicate with the housekeeper.

'By yourself?'

Leo sounded incredulous and Margo only just kept from rolling her eyes.

'Leo, I'm a grown woman—'

'You're also pregnant—'

'Pregnancy is not a disease.'

'You've been suffering from extreme morning sickness, Margo, and I've seen how dizzy you can get. What if something had happened?'

She quelled the lurch of alarm she felt at that thought. Just when she'd been coming to grips with her own fear Leo had managed to rake it all up again.

'I can't just stay in the villa, Leo, like some knocked-up Rapunzel in her tower. I'll go mad.'

She heard a snort of laughter from behind her and turned around.

'Knocked-up Rapunzel?' Leo repeated, a smile tugging at his mouth. 'That presents quite an image.'

Margo smiled back. She'd missed this kind of banter so much. The jokes and the teasing…the *lightness*. She needed it to combat the darkness she felt so often in herself. 'Well, that's how I feel. And I don't even have tons of beautiful blonde hair to compensate.'

'Your hair is beautiful,' Leo said.

And just like that he dropped the banter, replacing it with an intent sincerity that made Margo's heart judder.

'I always enjoyed watching you when you unpinned it in the evening.'

All at once she had an image of Leo, gazing at her as she reached up to undo the chignon she normally kept her waist-length hair in. She pictured the hotel room, the candlelight casting flickering shadows across the wide bed. The moment's intimacy and expectation, the sheer eroticism of it…

It felt like a lifetime ago—and yet it also felt very real. She could remember exactly how it had felt when her hair had cascaded down her back and Leo had reached for her, taken her into his arms and pushed the heavy mass aside to kiss the tender nape of her neck…

She swallowed hard, not sure if she wanted to revel in the moment spinning out between them or move past it.

In the end Leo chose for her.

'I understand you needing to get out. But your mobile phone doesn't even work here—'

'Then perhaps I should get a new one. I can't be a prisoner, Leo.'

'I don't want you to be. I'll order you a phone today. I should have done it before. I'm sorry.'

She nodded wordlessly, still caught in the thrall of that moment, that memory.

'I was thinking,' Leo said abruptly, 'we should have a party. To welcome you properly and introduce you to the community. If you feel up to it.'

'I'm feeling much better. I'd like that.' Maybe a party would help her to meet people and finally start feeling a part of things.

* * *

Somewhat to Margo's surprise, Xanthe and Ava were excited about the party. They set a date, and contacted caterers, and sent out invitations to everyone in the local community.

And they took Margo shopping.

She resisted at first, because the thought of the two women fluttering around her like butterflies while she tried on dresses was alarming, to say the least. But they insisted and she finally gave in, driving with them into Amfissa one afternoon a few days before the party.

'You're not quite ready for maternity wear,' Ava said, casting a critical eye over Margo's neat bump. 'How far along are you, anyway?'

'Just over eighteen weeks,' Margo said.

The nausea had almost completely gone, and she was starting to feel a little more energetic and look a little less gaunt.

'You're so *thin*,' Xanthe said, envy audible in her voice. 'It seems like all Parisian women are thin. Do you ever eat?'

'Not lately,' Margo admitted, 'but normally, yes.'

Suddenly she thought of the mini-marshmallows she'd kept in her bag—her secret vice—and how Leo had known about them.

'You're smiling like a cat who just ate the cream,' Ava noted.

Margo shook her head. 'Just…remembering something.'

Which made the sisters exchange knowing looks.

And then Xanthe asked abruptly, 'So what is going on between you and Leo? Because obviously…' she gestured towards Margo's bump '…you've been together, but…' She trailed off as Ava gave her a quelling look.

Margo sighed. She'd come to realise that Ava and Xanthe were good-natured and well-intentioned, if a little interfering. They deserved the truth, or at least as much as she could tell them without betraying Leo's confidences.

'We were together. But things had...started to cool off. And then I became pregnant.'

'Accidentally?' Xanthe asked with wide eyes.

Ava snorted. 'Of course accidentally, *ilithia*.'

Margo recognised the Greek word for idiot; this wasn't the first time Ava had used it towards her younger sister and Leo, amused, had told her what it meant.

Ava turned to Margo. 'So you told Leo about the baby?'

'Yes. I never thought I'd have children, but—'

'Why not?' Xanthe interjected.

Margo hesitated. 'I suppose because I was focused on my career.' Which was no more than a half-truth. It was because she was afraid of loving and losing someone again—so desperately afraid.

Her hand crept to the comforting swell of her bump and Ava noticed the revealing gesture.

'Come on, let's try and find some dresses,' she said, and Margo was glad for the change in subject.

She spent a surprisingly enjoyable afternoon with both sisters once she'd got used to Xanthe's nosiness and Ava's bustling, bossy manner. She realised they were both fun to be around, and she could tell they actually cared about her. It almost felt like being part of a family—something she hadn't experienced since she'd been twelve years old, and even then not so much...

They finally all agreed on a dress of deep magenta that brought colour to Margo's face and complemented her dark eyes and hair. Its empire waist and swirling skirt drew attention away from her bump without hiding it completely.

'Understated, elegant, and just a little bit sexy,' Ava declared in satisfaction. 'Perfect. Leo will love it.'

And with a little thrill Margo realised she *wanted* Leo

to love it. She wanted to be beautiful to him again. A dangerous desire, perhaps, but still, caught in the happy glow of their shared afternoon, Margo didn't try and suppress it. Leo was her husband, after all. Why shouldn't she want him to find her attractive, desirable?

The night of the party, as she stood in front of the full-length mirror in her bedroom and gazed at her reflection, she wondered again just what Leo would think of her in this dress. She'd done her hair in its usual chignon but styled it a bit more loosely, so a few tendrils escaped to frame her face. She'd taken care with her make-up, making her eyes look bigger and darker with eyeliner and mascara, choosing a berry-red lipstick that matched her dress.

She looked, Margo thought, a bit more like her old self—the old Margo, who'd armed herself with make-up and designer clothes and stiletto heels. And yet she looked…softer, somehow. Her face was rounder, her bump was visible, and she didn't feel quite as guarded as she normally did.

Maybe living here in Greece with people all around her was softening her slowly. Changing her just a little. It was so different from the isolation she'd known for so long.

A knock sounded on the door that joined her bedroom to Leo's. He used it on occasion, to come and say goodnight to her, or talk with her about various matters. He always knocked first—always kept things formal and brief.

Now Margo cleared her throat before calling for him to enter.

'Are you—?'

He stopped as he caught sight of her, and Margo's breath dried in her throat as she looked at him. He wore a tuxedo, something she'd never actually seen him in before, and the crisp white shirt and black jacket was the perfect foil for his swarthy skin and ink-dark hair. The strong, clean lines of his jaw and cheekbones made Margo ache to touch him. And when she saw the blaze of desire in his eyes she felt as if a Roman candle had lit up inside her, fizzing and firing away.

'I was going to ask you if you were ready,' Leo said, his voice turning husky, 'but you obviously are. You look beautiful, Margo. Utterly enchanting.'

Colour touched her cheeks, and when she spoke her voice was almost as husky as his own. 'Thank you. You look…incredible.'

She blushed even more at this admission, and Leo's mouth quirked in a small smile. Margo could feel the tension snapping between them, but for once it was a good, exciting kind of tension. Sexual tension.

'Shall we?' he asked, and held out his hand.

Nodding, Margo took it.

Even though they'd been living as man and wife for a couple of weeks, they'd hardly ever touched. In this charged atmosphere the feel of his fingers sliding along her hand and then curling over her fingers made heat pool deep in Margo's belly.

Leo drew her out of the room and down the stairs towards the guests who were already arriving and milling in the foyer; the extra staff hired for the night circulated with trays of champagne and canapés.

The pooling desire she'd felt was replaced by a sudden lurch of nerves at the sight of all the people waiting to meet her, and maybe to judge her.

Leo gently squeezed her fingers. 'Chin up,' he said softly. 'You look beautiful and you are amazing.'

She glanced at him swiftly, surprise slicing through her at the obvious sincerity in his tone. What was happening between them? This certainly didn't feel businesslike.

But before she could say anything, or even think about

it any further, he was drawing her down the stairs and towards the crowd.

It had been a long time since Margo had socialised; morning sickness had kept her from doing anything but the bare minimum. Now, however, wearing a gorgeous dress, feeling beautiful and even cherished on Leo's arm, she felt some of her old sparkle return. And people, she found, were happy to welcome her.

A few glanced askance at her baby bump, but she suspected that most had already heard and come to terms with the new, unexpected addition to the Marakaios family. As Leo's wife, she was accepted by the people unequivocally, and it made her both relieved and grateful.

She felt even more so when Leo held his flute of champagne aloft and proposed a toast. 'To my lovely bride, Margo,' he said, his clear, deep voice carrying throughout the whole villa. 'May you welcome her and come to love her as I do.'

Margo smiled and raised her own glass of sparkling water, but his words caused a jolt of shock to run through her. *Love her*. He didn't, of course. She knew that. And yet for the first time she wondered what it would feel like if he did. If she loved *him*. If they had a proper marriage—real and deep and lasting.

A moot question, of course, because even if she wanted to risk her heart by loving Leo there was no guarantee that he would love her back. There were no guarantees at all—which was why it was better this way. They'd reached a level of amicability that was pleasant without being dangerous. She shouldn't want or seek more.

By the end of the evening her feet, in the black suede stilettos she'd had brought from Paris, were starting to ache, and she was definitely starting to wilt. Leo seemed to notice the exact moment she felt ready to call it a night, for in one swift movement he came to her side, putting his arm around her waist.

'You look tired. Why don't we retire?'

'I don't want to seem rude...'

'Greeks love a party. They will stay here till dawn unless I kick them out.'

Her mouth twitched in a smile and she let herself lean slightly into Leo's arm. Not enough for him to notice, or for it to matter. Just enough to feel the heavy, comforting security of it. To feel safe.

'So, are you going to boot them to the door?'

'I'll leave that to the staff. I'm going to come upstairs with you.'

And even though she knew he didn't mean it in *that* way, she still felt a shivery thrill run through her.

To her surprise, Leo didn't leave her at her bedroom door as he usually did at night, but came into the room behind her. Margo hadn't expected that, and she'd already started to undo her hair—the pins had been sticking into her skull all evening.

Suddenly self-conscious, she lowered her arms—and then froze at the sound of Leo's husky voice.

'Don't stop.'

In an aching rush she remembered how he'd told her he liked to watch her unpin her hair. It felt even more intimate, even more erotic, now that she knew he liked it. Slowly, her heart starting to thud, she reached up and took the pins out of her hair one by one.

Leo didn't say anything, but she could hear him breathing...feel the very air between them tauten. The pins now removed, she gave her head a little shake and her hair came tumbling down her shoulders, all the way to her waist.

Leo gazed at her, his eyes blazing, and Margo stared back, every sense in her straining, her heart thudding hard.

'Margo…'

She heard a world of yearning in his voice and it made her tremble. She pressed a hand to her middle to stay the nerves that leapt like fish in her belly—and then realised they weren't nerves at all.

'*Oh…*'

'What?' Leo came towards her quickly, his voice sharp with concern. 'What is it?'

'I think…' Margo pressed her hand against her bump, a smile dawning across her face. 'I think I felt the baby kick.'

'You *did*?' Leo sounded incredulous, amazed, as if he'd never heard of such a thing.

Margo let out a little laugh as she felt that same insistent pulse of life. 'Yes! I just felt it again!' She looked up at him, beaming, as amazed as he was. 'It feels so *funny*. There's actually a person inside me!'

He laughed then, and so did she, and then he reached out a hand—before staying it. 'May I?' he asked.

Margo nodded. She reached for his hand, pressing it to her bump, her hand on top of his. 'Wait,' she whispered, and they both stood there, still and transfixed, barely breathing.

It seemed an age, but then finally it came again: that funny little inward thump.

Leo let out an incredulous laugh. '*Theos*, I felt it! I really felt it.'

She looked up at him, still beaming, but the wide smile slid right off her face as she saw Leo's own joyful incredulity turn into something else. Something sensual.

The breath rushed from her lungs as he reached out one hand and slid it through her hair so his fingers curved around the nape of neck, warm and sure and seeking. He drew her slowly towards him and she came, one palm resting flat against his chest so she could feel the thud of his heart, as insistent as her own.

And then he kissed her, as she knew he would, his lips brushing hers once, twice, in a silent question. Without waiting for an answer—an answer she'd have given with every part of her body—he went deep, his tongue sliding into her mouth as he pulled her more closely to him, fitting their bodies together as much as her bump would allow.

The feel of his lips on hers…his hands on her body…his touch made every sense she had flare painfully alive as need scorched through her. She slid her hands up to clutch at his lapels and opened her mouth to his kiss, his tongue, felt the raw passion inside her kindle to roaring flame.

And then the baby kicked again—that determined little pulse—and Margo froze. Her thoughts caught up with the sensations rushing through her and that little kick reminded her just why they were here in the first place. The only reason they were here.

Leo, as attuned as ever to her emotions, broke off the kiss and stepped back. Margo couldn't tell a single thing from his expression. His gaze dropped to her bump and she wondered if he too were reminding himself of the real and only reason they'd got married.

The silence stretched on, and Margo could not think how to break it. Her emotions felt like a maelstrom, whirling inside her; she couldn't separate one from the other, couldn't articulate how she felt about anything.

In the end Leo broke it with a single word. 'Goodnight,' he said quietly, and then walked to the door that joined their bedrooms.

Margo was still standing in the centre of the room, one hand pressed to her bump, another to her kiss-swollen lips, as she heard the door click softly shut.

CHAPTER TEN

LEO PACED THE length of his bedroom and willed the blood in his veins to stop surging with the furious demand to taste Margo again. To bury himself inside her.

He let out a shuddering breath and sank onto the bed, dropping his head into his hands. *He'd come so close...*

But then she'd frozen, and he'd felt her emotional if not her physical withdrawal. No matter how sizzling their chemistry had once been, Margo had still chosen to reject him. And the way she'd stilled beneath his touch had felt like another rejection.

His hands clenched in his hair and he considered opening the door between their bedrooms and demanding his marital rights. They were husband and wife, and he knew Margo desired him—whether she wanted to or not. She was feeling better and the pregnancy was healthy—why shouldn't they enjoy each other?

But, no. He would not share Margo's bed until she wanted him to be there. Utterly.

And yet the evening had started so promisingly. He'd loved seeing Margo at the party, looking bright and beautiful, as much her old self as ever, reminding him of how interesting and articulate and sophisticated she really was. And when she'd drawn his hand to her bump and he'd felt their child kick… It had been the most intimate thing Leo had ever experienced.

The kiss had felt like a natural extension of that intimacy. He couldn't have kept himself from it if he'd tried—which he hadn't.

So what had gone wrong? What had spooked Margo?

Then, with a wince, Leo remembered the toast he'd given at the party. *'May you welcome her and come to love her as I do.'* He hadn't thought of the words before he'd said them; they'd simply flowed out of him, sounding so very sincere. But he'd assured Margo he didn't love her—just as she didn't love him. Had his toast frightened her off?

Had he meant those words?

It was a question he strove to dismiss. Things had become muddied with Margo. Their business arrangement was morphing into something more amicable and pleasant. And yet…*love*?

No. No, he wouldn't go there. He'd suffered enough rejection in his life—starting with his father's determination to exclude his second son. He didn't need more of it from a woman who had already made it clear what she wanted from this marriage.

The same thing he wanted. The *only* thing he'd let himself want. A safe, stable life for the child they had created.

The next morning Margo came into the breakfast room and hesitated in the doorway. Leo saw uncertainty flash across her features and forced himself to stay amicable, yet a little cool. They'd had breakfast together every morning since they'd been here and today would be no different.

'Good morning.' He rose from the table to pour the ginger tea he'd requested Maria to brew every breakfast time. 'Did you sleep well?'

'Yes, thank you.'

Margo sat across from him and spread out her napkin on her lap. Leo thought she looked paler than usual, with dark smudges under her eyes.

She must have caught him looking for she smiled ruefully and said, 'Actually, not really.'

'I'm sorry to hear that.' He handed her the tea and then returned to his seat before snapping open his newspaper. 'It's always hard to sleep after a party, I find.'

Such bland, meaningless conversation—and yet it provided a necessary kind of protection, a return to the way things needed to be.

'It wasn't because of the party, Leo,' Margo said.

He glanced up from the paper and saw her give him a direct look that stripped away his stupidly bland attempts at conversation, saw right into his soul.

'It was because of our kiss.'

Our kiss. Memories raced across his brain, jumpstarted his libido.

He took a sip of coffee and answered evenly. 'Yet you were the one who stopped it.'

'Actually, *you* were,' she answered.

'Semantics,' he returned. 'You were the one who stopped responding, Margo.'

'I know.' She looked down at her plate, her long, slender fingers toying with her fork, her face hidden.

'Why did you, as a matter of interest?' Leo asked, half amazed that he was asking the question. Did he really want to know the answer? 'It wasn't because you weren't interested. I could feel your desire, Margo. You wanted me.'

'I know,' she said softly. 'Whatever you think…whatever you believe…I've never stopped wanting you, Leo.'

'Ah, yes, of course,' he drawled sardonically. 'It's *loving* me you have a problem with.' *Damn it.* He had *not* meant to say that.

She looked up, her gaze swift and searching. 'But you don't love me, either.'

'No.' So why did he feel so exposed, so *hurt*? He let out a short, impatient huff of breath. 'I'm not sure why we're even having this conversation.'

'Because I think we're both trying to navigate this relationship,' Margo answered quietly. 'This marriage. And I'm not sure I know how to be businesslike with my husband.'

'You seem to be managing fine.'

'Maybe, but when you came into my room last night… when you felt the baby kick…it made me realise that we're actually going to be parents.' She let out a self-conscious laugh and continued, 'I knew it before, of course, but for a moment I had this image of us together with a child—giving it a bath, teaching it to ride a bike. Boy or girl, this baby is ours and we'll both love him or her. I know that. And I don't know where being businesslike fits in with that. With a family. The kind of family I want…that I've always wanted—' She broke off, averting her face.

Leo stared at her. 'Yet you're the one who has said you don't wish to be married, who viewed this marriage as a sacrifice,' he reminded her. Reminded *himself.* As much as he wanted to, he couldn't get past that. The real feelings, or lack of them, that she'd shown when he had proposed.

'I said that because I thought you'd hate me after what I said before,' Margo said. 'About there being someone else.'

'And why *did* you say that?' Leo challenged in a hard voice. 'Why did you choose to lie in such an abominable way?'

'I told you before. Because it was the only way I could think of to—to make you leave me.'

Everything in him had crystallised, gone brittle. 'Yes,

I remember. And why did you want me to leave you so much, Margo?'

She was silent—so terribly, damnably silent.

Leo reached for his fork and knife. 'I see,' he said quietly, and he was afraid he saw all too well. The brutal rejection of it, of *him*, was inescapable.

Margo had come to breakfast after a restless, sleepless night, determined to talk to Leo and, more than that, to come to an agreement. An arrangement. Even though the details remained vague in her head. She didn't want to be businesslike any more—didn't want this polite stepping around each other.

Yet what was the alternative? How did you engage your heart and mind and maybe even your soul without risking everything?

And she knew she wasn't ready to do that. She hadn't even been able to tell Leo that the real reason why she'd refused his marriage proposal was that she'd been so very afraid. Annelise… Her mother… The foster parents who had decided she wasn't what they wanted… So many had turned away, and she knew she couldn't take it if Leo did. Not if she'd given him her heart—fragile, trampled on thing that it was.

But her silence had led to this terrible strain, with Leo having turned back to his newspaper, his expression remote and shuttered.

'What are you doing today?' she blurted, and he looked up from the paper, not even a flicker of interest or emotion on those perfectly chiselled features.

'Working in the office, as usual.'

'I should probably arrange to go to Paris soon. I still need to finish things at Achat.'

'If you feel well enough,' he said, sounding uninterested. 'I don't see a problem with that.'

Margo stared at him, her heart sinking right down to her toes. She didn't want this. She'd come down this morning wanting to try to make things better, and she'd only made them worse.

'Leo, you gave me a tour of the villa, but I haven't seen the rest of the estate or the olive groves. Do you think you'd have time today to show me?'

There. That was her peace offering—her attempt at building some kind of bridge. She just hoped Leo would take the first step onto its flimsy surface.

He gazed at her, his eyes narrowed, and then gave a brief nod and folded up his newspaper. 'I suppose… I'll come back to the villa after lunch.'

Margo spent as much time getting ready for her tour of the olive groves as if it were a first date. Not that she'd had many of those. Both her short-lived and frankly disappointing relationships prior to Leo had made her wonder if she was even capable of a real, loving relationship. She certainly didn't have a lot of experience of them.

It was cold out, at just a little less than two weeks before Christmas, and Margo struggled to fit into her jeans. She couldn't zip them all the way up, and the button was a lost cause. She wore a tunic top of aquamarine cashmere that fell nearly to her knees and fitted snugly round her bump while hiding the undone zip and buttons.

She left her hair loose, which she rarely did, and put on a bit of eyeliner and lipstick. She didn't necessarily want to look as if she was trying too hard, but she definitely wanted Leo to notice.

Unfortunately he didn't say a word when she met him in the foyer, and Margo suppressed the flicker of disappointment she felt at his silence. Had she really expected him to compliment her? She was wearing *jeans*, for heaven's sake. Still, she noticed that Leo seemed terser than usual as they headed out into the bright, frosty afternoon.

'There isn't actually all that much to see in the olive groves at this time of year,' he remarked as they walked along the gravel road that went past his office and led to a pair of wrought-iron gates. 'The trees are bare, and they won't begin to bud until March.'

'I still want to see,' Margo said, trying to keep her tone upbeat. 'This is my home now, after all. I don't know the first thing about olive trees or oil or *any* of it.'

'You don't need to learn.'

So he really was rebuffing her.

'I *want* to learn, Leo. You told me you wanted me to be a part of things. That's what I'm trying to do.'

He stared at her, as inscrutable as ever, and she decided to try a different tack.

'Tell me about your childhood. Did you grow up playing hide-and-seek in these groves?'

They'd stepped through the gates and were now walking among the trees, the trunks twisted and gnarled, the branches stark and bare.

'A bit,' Leo answered. 'I grew up here, certainly.'

'Did you like it?' she asked, for she sensed more than reticence in Leo's reply, and wondered at his memories.

'I loved the olive trees,' he said after a moment. 'The white waxy blossoms, the dusty scent in summer, the nuttiness of the oil…' He shook his head. 'I probably sound ridiculous, but I love it all. I always have.'

So why, Margo wondered, did he sound so regretful? So *bitter*?

'It's a good thing you're in the olive oil business,' she said, and Leo gave her a rather tight smile.

'Yes.'

'Why,' Margo asked after a moment, as they walked between the bare trees, 'do I feel as if you're not telling me everything?'

'What do you mean?'

She shrugged, half afraid to press, yet wanting to know more about him. Wanting to keep building this bridge, flimsy as it seemed. 'When you talk about the trees, the business, you sound…tense.' She hesitated and then added, 'Almost angry.'

Leo was silent for a long moment, and the only sound was the wind soughing through the trees and making the branches rattle. 'I suppose,' he said finally, 'that's because I am. Or was, at least. I think I'm getting over it. I hope so, anyway.'

Leo's face gave nothing away, and yet Margo knew instinctively this was a big admission for him to make. 'Why, Leo?' she asked quietly. 'What happened?'

He sighed, shrugging and shaking his head at the same time. 'Just complicated family politics.'

'Tell me.'

He hesitated, then said, 'My grandfather started the business from scratch. He was a dustman before he scraped together enough drachmas to buy a bit of property, and he built it from there. We've always been so proud of how we came from nothing. How we built this empire with our own hands. First my grandfather, and then my father…'

He trailed off, frowning, and Margo dared to fill in, 'And now you?'

'Yes. But it didn't happen as seamlessly as that.'

'Your brother…?'

'Yes, my brother.' His face tightened. 'Antonios was my father's favourite. The oldest child and his heir…I suppose it was understandable.'

'It's *never* understandable,' Margo countered. 'If we have more children I won't favour one more than the other.'

He gave her a swift, blazing look. 'Do you *want* more children, Margo?'

'I...' She swallowed hard. More children to love. *More children to lose.* And yet a proper family—the kind of family she'd always longed for but had been afraid to have. Was afraid she didn't deserve. 'I don't know.'

He kept staring at her, his gaze searching and yet not seeming to find any answers, for eventually he looked away and resumed his story.

'Well, understandable or not, Antonios was the favourite. I didn't accept that, though. I tried—*Theos*—how I tried to make my father love me. Trust me—'

He broke off then, and Margo ached to comfort him. But she didn't, because everything about Leo was brittle and tense, and she had a terrible feeling—a fear—that he would shake her off if she tried to hug him as she wanted to.

'To make a long story short,' he continued finally, his voice brusque, 'he never did. He had a heart attack and he sent for Antonios—told him the truth about the business. He'd been involved in dodgy dealings for years, trying to make back the money he'd lost on bad investments. He was a hair's breadth away from losing everything. He made Antonios swear not to tell anyone...not even me.'

'And *did* he tell you?' Margo asked.

Leo shook his head. 'Not for ten years. Ten years of my not understanding, feeling cut off and kept in the dark. Well...' he shrugged and then dug his hands into his pockets '...I don't suppose I should have been very surprised. My father never trusted me with anything—why would he with the truth?'

'But your brother...?'

'Antonios didn't either. Not until I pushed and pushed

for him to say something—and then I think he only did because of Lindsay, his wife. She wanted an end to all the secrets, all the acrimony.'

'And *has* there been an end to it?' Margo asked.

'I…I don't know. We get along—more or less. Antonios resigned as CEO, as you know, and is happier working in investment management.'

'Are *you* happy?' Margo asked, and the question hung there, suspended, encompassing so much more than just the business.

'I don't know,' Leo said again, and he turned to look at her, his face more open and honest and vulnerable than she'd ever seen it before—even when he'd asked her to marry him. 'I don't know,' he said again, and it seemed like more than an admission. It seemed like a revelation… to both of them.

They started walking again, back towards the gates, neither of them speaking. This time, however, the silence didn't feel strained, Margo thought, more expectant. Although what she—or Leo—was waiting for, she had no idea.

The gates loomed ahead of them and Margo had the strange sensation that once they passed through them things would change. The spell of intimacy and honesty that had been cast over them amidst the trees would be broken.

She turned to tell Leo something of this—something of herself—but before she could say anything her foot caught on a twisted root and she pitched forward. The moment felt as if it lasted for ever, and yet no time at all, no time to try to right herself, or even to break her fall with her hands.

She fell hard onto her front, her belly slamming into the ground, her face and hands and knees scraped and stinging.

'*Margo—*' Leo's voice was sharp with alarm and even fear as he knelt at her side.

She got onto her hands and her knees, her heart thudding from the fall.

Leo put a hand on her shoulder. 'Are you all right? Let me look at you.'

Slowly, wincing from the bruises and scrapes, she eased back into a sitting position, the ground hard and cold beneath her.

'I think I'm okay,' she said, and pressed one hand to her belly, her fingers curving around her bump, willing the baby to give a little comforting kick in response to the silent question her hand was asking.

Then she caught Leo staring at her; his face was pale, his eyes wide, and he leaned forward, grabbing her arm.

'What—?' she began, but Leo was already sliding his phone out of his pocket and dialling 112, which she knew was the number in Greece for the emergency medical services. 'Leo, I'm okay,' she said.

And that was when she felt a sticky wetness between her thighs, and when she looked down she saw blood spreading across the hard earth.

CHAPTER ELEVEN

'No!' MARGO'S VOICE was hoarse as she stared at the blood on the ground, and then she let out a harsh, keening cry that tore at Leo's heart. '*No.* Leo—no, no, *no*—' Her voice caught and she struggled for a moment, every breath an effort as panic swamped her.

'I have an emergency medical situation,' he snapped into the phone. 'I need an ambulance at the Marakaios estate immediately.'

He tossed the phone aside and reached for Margo. She was rocking back and forth, her arms wrapped around her middle, her whole body trembling.

'Margo, breathe,' he commanded. 'Nice and even. It's going to be okay.'

She took a few hitched breaths, her shoulders shaking, and then finally managed to speak. 'Don't lie to me, Leo,' she said raggedly. 'Don't ever lie to me. It's *not* going to be okay. You can't know that.'

'You're bleeding,' he acknowledged steadily, 'but that doesn't mean anything is wrong with the baby.'

But Margo seemed barely to hear him. She shook her head, tears streaking down her face. 'This can't happen,' she whispered to herself. 'This *can't* happen. I won't let this happen again.'

Again? Leo's mind snagged on the word, but now was hardly the time to ask her what she meant.

'An ambulance will be here in a few minutes. I'm going to move you so it can reach you more easily.'

Gently he scooped her up into his arms and carried her out of the olive grove. He could see the blood staining her jeans and coat and his stomach roiled with fear. Margo had been right. He couldn't know if it was going to be okay.

Soon an ambulance came screeching and wailing up the drive. Leo saw his sisters and Maria crowd onto the villa's portico as he carried Margo towards the vehicle. A paramedic came out to help her onto a stretcher.

'Leo!' Xanthe cried, and he shook his head.

'I'll call you,' he promised, and then climbed into the ambulance with Margo.

She looked so vulnerable, lying there on the stretcher, her eyes huge and dark in her pale face, and she scrabbled for his hand, her fingers fragile and icy in his as the paramedic took her vitals and then asked Leo what had happened.

Leo gave the details as clearly and evenly as he could; he could feel Margo clinging to his hand, her breath coming in little pants as she tried to control her panic.

Dear God, he prayed, *let nothing have happened to the baby.*

The next half-hour was a blur as the ambulance took them to the hospital in Amfissa, and then to an examination room in the A&E. A doctor, brisk and purposeful, came in with an ultrasound machine while Margo lay on the examination couch.

'The first thing to do,' the doctor said in Greek, 'is a scan, so I can see what's going on.'

Leo translated for Margo and she nodded frantically, still clutching his hand.

The next few minutes, as the doctor set up the machine, seemed to last for ever. Leo watched as she spread cold, clear gel on Margo's belly and then pressed the wand against her bump. The silence that stretched on for several seconds was the worst thing he'd ever heard, and Margo gave a soft, broken little cry before turning her head away from the ultrasound screen. Tears snaked silently down her cheeks, and Leo felt the sting of tears in his own eyes.

This couldn't be happening.

'There it is,' the doctor said in Greek, and Leo stared in stunned disbelief as she pointed to the screen and the tiny heartbeat, still going strong.

'*Margo—*'

'She has a partial placenta praevia,' the doctor said, and Leo tried to listen as she explained how the placenta was covering the cervix and the fall had aggravated it, which had caused the bleeding.

He could barely take it in, however—all he could do was stare at that wonderful little pulsing assurance of life.

'Margo…' he said again and, touching her cheek, he turned her face to the screen.

She blinked, tears still slipping down her face, as she stared in confusion at the screen.

'It's okay,' he said softly. 'It really is okay.'

Smiling, the doctor turned up the volume, and that wonderful, whooshing, galloping sound of the baby's heartbeat filled the room. Leo thought Margo would be relieved, that she might even smile or laugh, but as she heard the sound of the heartbeat her face crumpled and she collapsed into sobs, her shoulders shaking with their force.

Leo didn't think past his overwhelming need to comfort her. He leaned over and put his arms around and she buried her face in his shoulder as her whole body shook and trembled.

Quietly the doctor turned the machine off and wiped the gel from Margo's bump. 'She should stay overnight—just for observation,' she told Leo. 'Tomorrow we can do another scan to see how the bleeding looks and if the placenta has moved any more.'

Leo nodded wordlessly. He'd have to process all that later; the only thing he could think about now was Margo.

Eventually she eased back from him and wiped the tears from her face, managing the wobbliest of smiles. A nurse came to transfer her to a room, and Leo called his sisters while Margo showered and changed into a hospital gown. When he came back into the room she was lying in bed, her hair brushed and her face washed, but her eyes still looked puffy and red from crying.

He sat on the edge of her bed and took her hand. 'The doctor said you have a partial placenta praevia,' he said. 'To be honest, I can't remember what that means, exactly, but I'll arrange for a doctor who speaks English to talk to you about it.'

'I know what it means,' Margo said.

She sounded exhausted, emotionally spent, and Leo squeezed her fingers. 'The important thing is the baby is okay.'

'Yes. For now.'

She bit her lip, and Leo saw her eyes glisten with the sheen of new tears.

'There's no reason to be afraid, Margo—'

'Oh, Leo, there's every reason.' She leaned her head back against the starchy white pillow and closed her eyes. '*Every* reason.'

'I don't understand…'

He thought once more of how she'd said she didn't want this to happen *again*. He wanted to ask her what she'd meant, but he knew Margo was feeling too fragile now for such an emotional conversation.

'Is there something you're not telling me?' he asked instead, needing to know that much.

She opened her eyes and shook her head. 'Nothing that really matters.'

'Then why—?'

'I'm just so afraid.' She bit her lip. 'I'm *always* so afraid. That's why I didn't want to have children.'

He stared at her in confusion, trying to understand what she meant. He thought of when he'd met her in that hotel bar, looking sassy and smart in a black wrap cocktail dress, her long legs encased in sheer tights, a stiletto dangling from one slim foot. She'd looked like the most fearless person he'd ever met, and she'd always seemed that way to him: breezing into hotel rooms, giving him a naughty smile, shrugging out of her dress with confidence and ease.

He'd liked that about her, had enjoyed her sense of confidence. But now he wondered. Since Margo had come back into his life he'd wondered what she'd been hiding, what secrets she had. Had that breezy confidence all been an *act?*

'You don't need to be afraid,' he said, squeezing her fingers.

But, withdrawing her hand from his, Margo just turned away and said nothing.

Frustration bit hard but he forced himself not to demand answers or explanations. Once again he was being kept in the dark about something. It felt like another kind of rejection, because Margo obviously didn't trust him with whatever truth she was keeping from him. But he wouldn't press. He wouldn't beg.

Reluctantly he eased himself off the bed. 'Is there anything I can get you?' he asked. 'Something to drink or eat? Or something from the villa? Your own pyjamas or clothes?'

She was still looking away from him, her hair brushing her cheek. 'No, thank you.'

He hated how formal she was being, even though that morning he'd decided that was just how he wanted it. Things had changed. Both their conversation in the olive grove and the terrifying events afterwards had changed him. And they'd changed Margo too—but not in a way he liked or wanted.

Everything about her, from her brittle voice to the way she wouldn't look at him, made him think she wanted him to go. But he wasn't going to leave her here alone, whatever she wanted, so he settled himself into a chair opposite the bed and waited.

Neither of them spoke for a very long time, and eventually Margo drifted off to sleep.

When Margo awoke the room was dark, and panic doused her in an icy wave. She struggled upright, one hand going to her middle, curving over the reassuring bump even as the remnants of the nightmare she'd been having clung to her consciousness.

'Leo—'

'I'm here.'

In the darkness she couldn't see him, but she felt his hand come and close over hers. Even so she couldn't stop shivering.

'I had the most awful dream.' Her voice choked and her throat closed. She'd dreamed about Annelise—something she hadn't done in a very long time. 'It was so terrible—'

'It was just a dream, Margo,' Leo said, his voice soft and steady. 'It wasn't real. Everything's all right. The baby's all right.'

She nodded and gulped, wanting, *needing* to believe him and yet not quite able to do so. The dream had been real once upon a time. She'd relived the worst memory she had in her nightmare, and she was so afraid of it happening again. But Leo couldn't understand that because she hadn't told him.

'Don't leave me,' she whispered, and he squeezed her hand.

'I won't.'

But she needed more than just his reassurance; she craved the comfort of his touch. 'Leo…' she began, and then, thrusting any awkwardness aside, she blurted, 'Would you hold me?'

Leo didn't answer, and Margo braced herself for his refusal—because they didn't have that kind of relationship. That kind of marriage.

Then wordlessly he rose from the chair and peeled back the covers on her bed. He kicked off his shoes and slid into the narrow bed next to her, pulled her carefully into his arms.

Margo wrapped herself around him, burying her face in his neck, breathing in the clean, comforting scent of him. She'd needed this—needed him—more than she could ever have put into words.

He didn't say anything, just held her, one hand stroking her hair, until she felt the icy panic that had frozen her insides start to recede, the nightmare begin to fade. Her breathing evened out and her body relaxed into his embrace.

Lying there, safe in his arms, she felt a creeping sense of guilt for how much she'd kept from him. He'd been her rock since she'd fallen in the olive grove—he'd never left her, never wavered for an instant, offering her unconditional encouragement and support.

The realisation brought a lump to Margo's throat and she pressed her face more snugly against the hollow of his neck, breathing him in more deeply…

She must have fallen asleep again, for when she woke up the pale grey light of early dawn was filtering through the curtains and Leo was still in her bed.

Margo eased back to look at him. His eyes were closed, his thick, dark lashes fanned out on his cheeks. His jaw was rough with morning stubble, which made his lips look all the more lush and mobile and eminently kissable.

He was still in his clothes from yesterday, his shirt unbuttoned at the throat, his tie tossed on a chair. Margo felt as if a fist had wrapped around her heart and squeezed.

Then the door to the room opened and a nurse wheeled a machine in. 'Time to take your vitals,' she said cheerfully, and Margo blinked in surprise.

'You speak English?'

'Yes, Kyrie Marakaios requested that someone who could speak English attend to you. Or French, he said. But no one spoke good enough French.' She gave a little smile and a shrug, and then took out a blood pressure cuff and wrapped it around Margo's arm.

Leo had woken up and was now easing himself to a sitting position, wincing slightly at the stiffness in his body from spending a night fully clothed on a hospital bed. His hair was rumpled and he blinked sleep out of his eyes before turning to Margo.

'Are you all right?' he asked quietly.

She nodded. The fear that had gripped her so tightly yesterday had now eased a little, thanks to Leo.

He rose from the bed and while the nurse took Margo's blood pressure and temperature he left the room in search of coffee and a shave.

'The doctor will visit in a little while, for another ultrasound,' the nurse told her. 'And in the meantime you can have breakfast.'

Margo nodded, and a few minutes later Leo returned with two cups—one of coffee and another of ginger tea.

'Where on earth did you get *that*?' Margo asked as he handed her the cup.

'I make sure to always have some on me. Just in case.'

'You're so thoughtful,' she said, almost wonderingly.

Leo laughed ruefully. 'Don't sound so surprised!'

'I *am* surprised,' she admitted. 'There haven't…there haven't been that many people in my life who have been thoughtful.'

Leo frowned and Margo looked away. She wasn't ready to tell him any more than that, but she could tell he had questions. Questions he wanted answers to.

Before he could ask anything the door opened again, and a smiling woman brought in a breakfast tray.

After breakfast the doctor came with the ultrasound machine, and they both silently held their breath as she set it up—until the image of their baby came onto the screen, still kicking up a storm.

'Oh, I can feel that!' Margo exclaimed, one hand pressed to her bump. 'I hadn't felt anything since I fell, but I felt that.'

'This little one doesn't like being poked,' said the doctor, who also spoke English, with a smile. 'Everything looks fine. You'll have your twenty-week scan in a few days, and we'll check on the placenta praevia then.' Smiling, the woman put the machine away and Margo pulled down her shirt. 'You're free to go.'

It wasn't until she was dressed and they were back in the car, heading towards the estate, that Leo turned to her, his expression serious.

'Margo, we need to talk…'

Her body went tense and she turned to stare blindly out of the window.

'What are you not telling me?' Leo asked, his voice quiet but insistent. 'Because there's something.'

'It doesn't matter.'

'It *does* matter. It matters because in the hospital you were terrified—'

'Of course I was!' She turned to look at him. 'Leo, I was afraid I was losing my baby.'

'*Our* baby,' he corrected quietly, and Margo bit her lip. 'Don't shut me out, Margo.'

She turned back to the window without replying, and they drove in silence all the way back to the Marakaios estate.

CHAPTER TWELVE

WHEN THEY ARRIVED at the villa Leo helped Margo out of the car, one hand on her elbow as he guided her inside.

Xanthe, Ava and Maria all met them in the foyer.

'You're all right?' Ava asked, her face pinched with anxiety.

'Yes—and, more importantly, the baby is all right,' Margo said, and smiled when Maria muttered a prayer of thanksgiving and crossed herself.

'I'm going to get Margo upstairs,' Leo cut across his sisters' anxious chatter. 'It's been an incredibly long twenty-four hours, and I don't think either of us slept well last night.'

Actually, Margo had slept better than she had in months, wrapped in Leo's arms. But she could imagine Leo had spent a considerably less comfortable night, cramming his large body onto the narrow bed, still in his suit.

They went upstairs, and as Margo came into her bedroom she breathed a sigh of relief. She wanted to crawl into the big, soft bed and stay there for about a million hours—good night's sleep or not.

Behind her, she heard Leo close the door. 'I need to shower and change,' he said, 'and I imagine you'd like to freshen up. And then we'll talk.'

His tone was implacable, leaving no room for arguments. Still, Margo tried. 'I'm very tired, Leo—'

'There will be plenty of time for you to rest today. But I won't let you put me off, Margo.' He hesitated, seeming to want to say more, but then simply turned and left the room.

Margo went into the bathroom, stepping into the huge two-person shower with its marble sides and gold fixtures. As the water streamed over her body she had a sudden image of Leo joining her there. They'd showered together a few times during their stolen weekends away, but that felt like a lifetime ago. She felt like a different person from the insouciant, carefree career woman she'd been back then, embarking on a no-strings affair.

But then she *was* a different person—because that carefree woman had been nothing more than a part she'd played, a mask she'd worn. She hadn't dared try to be anything else. Anything deeper or more lasting.

In just a few minutes Leo was going to demand answers, and if she was brave enough she would drop that mask for ever and tell him everything. She knew he deserved to know.

She rested her head against the cool marble, willing herself to be strong enough for that kind of hard honesty.

A few minutes later she was dressed in a pair of loose yoga pants and a soft hoodie, curled up on the window seat that overlooked the villa's gardens, the grass now coated with a thick rime of frost.

Leo tapped once on the door that joined their bedrooms before poking his head in and then coming through completely. His hair was damp from his shower, and he wore a soft grey tee shirt and faded jeans that were moulded perfectly to his muscular legs. Wordlessly he walked over and joined Margo on the window seat.

Neither of them spoke for a long moment; the only

sound was the wind rattling the bare branches of the trees outside.

Finally Margo spoke, and each word felt laborious, even painful. 'I'm not who you think I am.'

'Who do you *think* I think you are?' Leo asked quietly.

'The woman you met in that bar. That glamorous, confident, sexy woman.' She let out a shaky laugh. 'Not that I'm trying to be arrogant, but that's how I wanted to be… to seem.'

Leo was silent for a moment, then finally he asked, 'Who are you, then?'

'A street rat from Marseilles.' She glanced at him, expecting to see if not disgust then at least surprise. But Leo looked completely unfazed.

'How did a "street rat from Marseilles" end up as a confident career woman in Paris?' he asked after a moment.

'Luck and hard work, I suppose.' She tucked her hair behind her ears and gazed out at the wintry afternoon. 'But I've always felt like a street rat inside.'

'That doesn't mean you *are*, Margo. I don't think anyone feels like the person they present to the world all the time.'

She pretended to look shocked. 'You mean you *don't* feel like an arrogant, all-powerful CEO all the time?'

He smiled and gave a little shrug. 'Well, obviously I'm the exception.'

She laughed at that, and then shook her head. 'Oh, Leo.' She let out a weary sigh, a sound of sadness. 'If you knew about my childhood…'

'Then tell me,' he said.

And although his voice was soft she knew it was a command. A command she should obey, because she'd already come to the decision that she needed to tell him the truth. But truth was a hard, hard thing.

'I grew up one step away from the street,' she began

slowly. 'And sometimes not even that. My mother was a drug addict. Crystal meth—although I didn't realise that until later. But it…the drug…controlled her life.'

Now, surely, he would look shocked. But when Margo looked at him his expression was still calm, although his mouth had pulled down at the corners with sympathy.

'I'm sorry.'

'So am I.' She let out a wobbly laugh that trembled into a half-sob. 'Oh, God, so am I.'

'Was she able to care for you?'

'No, not really, and sometimes not at all. At the beginning, yes. Before she became an addict. At least I think she did. I survived, anyway. But my father left when I was four—I only have a few fuzzy memories of him.'

'That must have been hard.'

'Yes.'

The few fuzzy memories she had were precious—of a man who'd pulled her into a bear hug and swung her in the air. *Why* had he left? It was a question that had tormented her for years. How could a man walk away from his family? Had she not been lovable enough?

'After he left my mother went very much downhill.'

She lapsed into silence then, because she did not want to tell him how grim it had been. The sheltered housing, the stints in various homeless shelters, the weeks when she'd been taken away from her mother and sent from one foster home to another. Some of them had been good, some of them mediocre, and some of them had been very bad. But always, in the end, she'd been brought back for her mother to try again, having promised she'd stay clean, and for a few days, sometimes a few weeks, she had.

Life during those periods had been normal, if fragile, and sometimes Margo would begin to believe it was going to be okay this time. Then she'd come home from school to find her mother strung out, or manically high, the promises all broken, and the whole cycle would start once more.

Until Annelise. But she really didn't want to talk about Annelise.

'Margo?' Leo prompted softly. 'Tell me more. If she couldn't care for you, how did you survive?'

She shrugged. 'Sometimes not very well. I was in and out of foster homes my whole childhood. When I was old enough I learned to take care of myself.'

'And how old was that?' Leo asked in a low voice.

'Seven…eight? I could use the gas ring in our bedsit and I could make basic meals. I got myself to school most days. I managed.'

'Oh, Margo.' He shook his head, reached for her hand. 'Why didn't you tell me this before?'

'I don't talk about my childhood to anyone,' she said, her voice thickening. 'Ever. It's too awful. And in any case, Leo, we didn't have that kind of relationship.'

His fingers tightened on hers. 'Do we now?'

Her heart lurched at the thought. 'I…I don't know.'

Which was what he had said to her yesterday morning. So much uncertainty, for both of them, and yet here she was confessing. Trying.

'Tell me more about your childhood,' Leo said after a moment.

She closed her eyes briefly. 'I could go into details, but I'm sure you can guess. It…it wasn't pretty, Leo.'

'I know that.' He was silent for a moment, his fingers still entwined with hers. 'But there's something more, isn't there? Something you're not telling me?'

'Yes.' She took a deep breath. 'When I was eleven, my mother had a baby. My half-sister. There was no father ever in the picture.' Another breath to keep herself going. 'Her name was Annelise.'

'Was?' Leo said softly, his fingers tightening on hers. 'What happened to her?'

'She...she died.'

She closed her eyes against the memories, but they came anyway. Annelise cuddled up to her in her bed, one chubby hand resting on her chest. Annelise toddling towards her with a big toothy grin, hands outstretched as she called Margo 'Go-Go'. Annelise with her arms wrapped around her neck, her cheek pressed to Go-Go's.

'I'm so sorry, Margo.'

'My mother was lucky not to have Annelise taken away from her right at the beginning,' she said, the words just barely squeezed out. 'With her history. But we'd flown under the radar for a couple of years by then. I was managing to get myself to school, and my mother seemed like she could control her addiction.'

She held up a hand to stop Leo saying anything, although he hadn't even opened his mouth.

'Which is ridiculous, I know, because of course an addiction can't be controlled. But she...she functioned, at least, and then when she found out she was pregnant she cleaned herself up for a while—enough for Annelise to be born and brought home.'

'And then?'

'As soon as Annelise was home she lost interest. I didn't mind, because I took care of her. I *loved* taking care of her.'

'But you had school—'

'I stopped going to school. I had to, for Annelise's sake. I told them we were moving, and nobody bothered to check. It was easy. Honestly, if you don't want to be noticed by the authorities it can be remarkably easy.'

'And so you stayed home and took care of Annelise?' Leo was silent for a moment. 'What did you do for money?'

'We got a little bit from the government. And my mother

would sometimes…' She hesitated, not wanting to admit just what her mother had done to score her drugs, but Leo must have guessed because his mouth tightened.

'She found a way to get money?' he surmised.

She nodded. 'Yes.' And then, because now that she'd started the truth-telling she felt she needed to say it all, she blurted, 'She sold herself. To men. For money.'

Leo nodded, his jaw tense, and Margo wondered what he thought of her now. In and out of foster homes, her mother a prostitute… She hated him knowing it.

'So what happened to you and Annelise?'

'I was her mother,' she whispered. 'I did everything for her. *Everything.*' She blinked rapidly and managed, 'She called me Go-Go.'

She stared down at her lap, at their entwined hands. And she thought of Annelise—her soft baby's hair, her gurgle of laughter.

How, after seventeen years, could it still hurt so much?

'How did she die?' Leo asked quietly.

'The flu. *The flu.*' Her voice choked and a tear slipped down her cheek. 'She just had a fever at first. I was taking care of her. I gave her some medicine and had her sleep in my bed, but…' She drew in a gasping breath. 'The fever spiked, and I was so scared, but I knew if I took her to hospital the authorities would get involved and they might take her away. I couldn't bear that, so I just bathed her in cool water and gave her more medicine.'

'And then…?' Leo asked softly.

'And then she started having convulsions. I begged my mother to take her to hospital then, but she…she wasn't herself.' She'd been high on drugs, barely aware of her children. 'So I took her myself. I carried her to the hospital in my arms. When I got there a nurse took her from me. She…she was already dead.'

She bowed her head, the memory and the pain and the guilt rushing through her.

'It was my fault, Leo. My fault she died.'

She'd never said those words aloud—never even admitted her guilt to herself. And saying it now made her feel both empty and unbearably full at the same time. She bowed her head and tried to will back the tears.

'Oh, Margo.' Leo's arms came around her and he pulled her towards him, her cheek against his chest. 'I'm so, so sorry.'

He didn't speak for a moment and she simply rested there, listening to the steady thud of his heart, letting the grief subside.

'It *wasn't* your fault, you know. You were twelve. You never should have had to bear that kind of responsibility.'

'I wasn't a child. And it *was* my fault. If I'd gone to the hospital earlier they could have given her antibiotics. Brought her fever down. Maybe she'd have been taken away, but she'd still be alive.' She spoke flatly, dully, knowing it was the truth and that nothing Leo could say would change it.

'What happened after that?' he asked after a moment. His arms were still around her, her cheek still against his chest.

'I was put into foster care—a few different families.'

She spoke diffidently, not wanting to admit all the terrible details. The foster mother who had dragged her by the hair into the bathroom because she'd said Margo was dirty. The family who had left her, at fourteen years old, in front of the council offices with nothing but a cardboard suitcase because they hadn't wanted her any more.

'It was tough for a few years,' she allowed. 'I missed Annelise so much… I acted out. I was hard to deal with.' And so people had chosen *not* to deal with her.

'When I was sixteen,' she continued after a moment, 'I finally calmed down. I stayed with a family for a year. They were good to me. They helped me find a job, saw me settled.'

'Are you still in touch with them?'

'No. It wasn't that kind of a relationship. They had a lot of different foster kids. I was just one of many. We wrote letters for a while, but…' She gave a little shrug. 'I am grateful to them. And really,' she continued quickly, 'I don't blame anyone except myself. The people who fostered me all tried their hardest. They didn't *have* to take children in. They were doing their best. And I really was difficult. I can't blame anyone but myself for that.'

'But you were a *child*,' Leo protested, 'in an incredibly difficult situation.'

'Yes, but I was mature for my age. I'd had to be. I could have…controlled myself.' Except she hadn't wanted to. She'd been wild with grief, wanting and needing to strike out. To hurt someone as she'd been hurting.

'And this is why you're so afraid now of something happening to the baby?' Leo said slowly. 'Because of what happened to Annelise?'

She nodded. 'I know it's not rational, but everyone I know has left me at one time or another. And Annelise… losing Annelise was by far the worst. I don't think I could survive something like that again, Leo. I really don't think I could.'

'You won't have to.'

'But you can't know—'

'I don't have a crystal ball to predict the future, no.' Leo took her chin his hand, turning her face so he could look her in the eye. 'But do you believe me, Margo, when I tell you I will do everything in my power—absolutely everything—to keep you and our child safe and healthy? I won't let you down, I swear to you. You can trust me.'

'Thank you,' she whispered, and although she didn't know if she had the strength to believe him she was still glad he'd said it.

Then, simply because it felt right, she leaned forward, closing the small space between them, and brushed her lips with his. It was barely more than a peck—a kiss that wasn't sexual or even romantic, but something else entirely. Something deeper and more tender.

Leo stilled under her touch, and then he eased back, his expression serious. 'Thank you for telling me. For trusting me that much.'

'I'm sorry I didn't before.'

'Like you said, we didn't have that kind of relationship.'

And did they now? Margo still didn't know. She didn't know what she was capable of, or what Leo wanted.

'You should rest,' Leo said as he stood up from the window seat. 'It's been a very long couple of days.'

'Yes...'

But she didn't feel tired, and after he'd left she paced the room restlessly, her mind starting to seethe with doubt and worry. She'd just unloaded a huge amount of emotional baggage onto Leo. When they'd struck their business deal he hadn't expected to have to cope with all that. What if he decided she was too much work? Or if he withdrew emotionally rather than deal with all the neurotic fears Margo had just confessed? Going back to being businesslike would be even harder and more painful now she'd confessed so much.

Tired with the circling questions she knew she couldn't answer, she decided to keep busy instead of simply pacing and worrying. She went to the adjoining bedroom that was meant to be a nursery and started sketching ideas to transform it into a space for a baby.

It had been weeks since she'd exercised her mind or her creativity, and it felt good to think about something other than the current anxieties that revolved around Leo and the baby. To remember that she'd had a career, one she'd enjoyed, and could still put to use, if only in this small way.

And as she sketched and planned she felt her uncertainties fall away, as if she were shedding an old skin, and she knew that she wanted to move forward from the past, from the pain. She wanted to move forward with Leo and have a real marriage. A loving one.

If she dared.

CHAPTER THIRTEEN

IN THE DAYS after Margo told him about her childhood Leo found himself going over what she'd said and connecting the dots that before had seemed no more than a scattered, random design of inexplicable behaviour.

Now he was starting to understand why Margo had decided to marry for the sake of their child.

After a childhood like hers, he could see how the stability of a family life was something she would want to provide for her child…even if they didn't love each other.

Except that basis was one Leo realised he could no longer assume. *Did* he love Margo? *Could* he love her? He certainly admired her resilience and her strength of spirit, her devotion to their unborn child. He was still deeply attracted to her, God knew. And if he let himself…if he stopped guarding his heart the way he suspected Margo was guarding hers…

Could this businesslike marriage become something more? Did he even want that? Margo had rejected him once. He understood why now, but it didn't mean she wouldn't do it again.

Things at least had become easier between them, and more relaxed: they shared most meals and chatted about ordinary things, and Margo had shown him her preliminary designs for the nursery, which he'd admired.

They were rebuilding the friendship they'd had before his marriage proposal, and this time it was so much deeper, so much more real.

One morning at breakfast Leo told her that Antonios and his wife Lindsay would be coming after Christmas for a short visit.

'Are you looking forward to that?' she asked, her dark, knowing gaze sweeping over him.

'Yes, I think I am,' Leo answered slowly.

He hadn't seen his brother since right after his mother's funeral, when Antonios and Lindsay had moved to New York and Leo had taken the reins of Marakaios Enterprises. He and Antonios had made peace with each other, but it was an uneasy one, and although they'd emailed and talked on the telephone since then Leo didn't know how it would feel to be in the same room, to rake over the same memories.

'It will be nice to meet some more of your family,' Margo said, breaking into his thoughts. 'Sorry I can't return the favour.'

She spoke lightly, but he saw the darkness in her eyes, knew she was testing him, trying to see how he felt about what she'd told him now that he'd had time to process it. Accept it.

And what he felt, Leo knew, was sadness for Margo. Regret that he hadn't known sooner. And a deep desire to make it better for her.

'We have all the family we need right here,' he said, and she blinked several times before smiling rather shyly.

'What a lovely thing to say, Leo.'

'It's true.'

'It's still lovely.'

That afternoon they headed into Amfissa for Margo's twenty-week scan. The last time they'd come to the hospital they'd been in an ambulance, filled with panic and fear. Leo saw the vestiges of both on Margo's face as he drove into the hospital car park and knew she was remembering. Hell, he was too.

The panic didn't leave Margo's face or Leo's gut until they were in the examination room and they could see their baby kicking on the screen.

The technician spent a long time taking measurements, checking the heart and lungs, fingers and toes. Leo held Margo's hand the whole time.

'Everything looks fine,' she said, and they both sagged a bit with relief. 'The placenta is starting to move, so hopefully the praevia will clear up before delivery. But we'll keep an eye on it. If it doesn't move completely by thirty weeks we'll have to talk about a scheduled Caesarean section.'

Margo nodded, her face pale. Leo knew she would do whatever it took to keep their baby safe and healthy, although such an operation was hardly ideal.

'Do you want to know the sex?' the technician asked. 'Because I can tell you. But only if you want to know.'

Leo and Margo looked at each other, apprehensive and excited.

'Could you write it down?' Leo asked. 'And put it in an envelope? Then we can open it together.'

'On Christmas Day,' Margo agreed, clearly getting into the spirit of the thing. 'A Christmas present to both of us.'

He smiled at her, and she smiled back, and Leo felt a kind of giddy excitement at the thought of knowing—and of knowing together.

Margo was determined to have a wonderful Christmas. The Christmases of her childhood had been unmarked, simply another day to survive. As an adult she'd decorated her apartment, and she and Sophie had exchanged presents, but that was as far as the celebrations had gone. Now, with a home and family of her own, she wanted to go all-out.

Leo told her that they'd never made much of Christmas either, when he was a child. In the Greek Orthodox church Easter was by far the greater holiday. Besides eating a grand meal on Christmas Day, and exchanging presents on January the sixth, Christmas passed by most Greek households virtually unnoticed.

'But I think we have much to celebrate this year,' he said, 'so I wouldn't mind changing things.'

So Margo did.

She wanted to keep the Greek spirit of things, and tried her hand at different Christmassy Greek treats: *melomakarona*, honey-dipped cookies stuffed with nuts, and *kourambiedes*, cookies dusted with powdered sugar. She and Maria made loaves of *christopsomo*—a round loaf decorated on the top with a cross, one of which adorned just about every Christmas table in Greece.

She gathered evergreen and pine boughs from around the estate and decorated the mantels and banisters; soon the whole villa smelled like a forest.

Leo brought in a Christmas tree and Margo made dough ornaments with Timon when Parthenope came to visit, enjoying the time with her husband's nephew and imagining how one day it would be her own child at her side.

It still seemed too good to be true, too wonderful to trust that it would actually happen. But with each day that passed she felt her faith in the future grow stronger…even as she wondered about herself and Leo.

Things were better, certainly, and far from businesslike. But they hadn't actually talked about the future, or what they felt for each other, and Margo wasn't brave enough to be the first one to confess that her feelings were growing and turning to love. She hardly wanted to admit it to herself, afraid that the fragile happiness they'd found would shatter into a million pieces…just as it had before.

In any case, there was still much to enjoy.

They all went into Amfissa on Christmas Eve for a midnight service. The Byzantine *kalandas* were different from the traditional songs and hymns Margo knew, but she liked them all the same.

Afterwards Ava and Xanthe retired to their rooms, and once she and Leo were alone in the sitting room, a fire crackling in the hearth and the Christmas tree glowing with fairy lights, Leo took an envelope out of his pocket.

'Shall we?'

'It's not Christmas yet,' Margo protested, even as she felt a tremulous thrill of excitement.

'It's after midnight.' Leo sat cross-legged on the thick rug in front of the fire and patted the space next to him. 'We'll open it together, so we can see at the same time.'

'All right,' Margo said, and a little bit awkwardly, because of her growing bump, sat next to him on the rug.

Wordlessly they opened the envelope, their fingers brushing as they withdrew the single slip of paper and read the single sentence in English the technician had written there.

It's a...boy!

'A boy…' Margo repeated wonderingly.

She felt jolted, almost unsettled. She'd been excited to find out the sex of their baby, but now that she knew it, it made things more real and less real at the same time.

She put both hands to her bump. 'A son. We're going

to have *a son.*' She glanced at Leo, who looked as gobsmacked as she felt. 'Are you happy?'

'I'm…overjoyed.' He put one hand over hers, on top of her bump. 'What about you?'

'Yes. It's strange, but it seems so hard to believe.'

'I know what you mean. But you're not…you're not disappointed?'

'Disappointed? Why would I be?'

'Because…because of Annelise.'

Just the name caused a little ripple of pain to go through her, but no more than that. Her hands curved more possessively around her bump. 'A baby girl wouldn't have replaced Annelise, Leo.'

'I know. Nothing can replace her. But it might have eased things, a bit.'

'No, it's better this way. A whole new start, for all of us.'

She caught her breath, her heart starting to thud as she realised just how much she meant that. How much she wanted it.

And Leo must have understood that, because Margo saw his eyes darken and his gaze move to her mouth.

'Margo…' he said, and then he kissed her. Softly, one hand cradling her face, the other still resting on her bump.

It was the most perfect moment, the most intimate and tender thing she'd ever experienced.

Then Leo broke away. 'I want you,' he said bluntly, and the simply stated fact caused a tremor to run through her. 'I want you very badly. But only…only if you want me.'

The vulnerability on his face made her ache. Those awful words she'd flung at him so many months ago still had the power to hurt.

She raised her hand to his cheek, cradling his face just as he'd cradled hers. 'I want you, Leo. I want you very much.'

'And it's safe…?'

'The doctor said it was.' She gave a small smile. 'And we don't need to worry about birth control.'

He laughed softly and kissed her again, this time holding nothing back, his tongue and lips causing a symphony of sensation inside her as beautiful and wondrous as any *kalanda* they'd sung that night.

'We could go upstairs,' Leo whispered, and he moved from her lips to her shoulder, kissing the curve of her neck as his hand found the warm swell of her breast, one thumb running over its already taut and aching peak.

Letting out a shudder of longing, Margo glanced at the crackling fire, the Christmas tree sparkling with lights. The house stretched all around them, quiet and dark.

'No, let's stay here,' she whispered, and began to unbutton Leo's shirt.

It felt like a wedding night, with the lights and the fire and the quiet sacredness of what they were doing.

Leo stilled under her touch as she finished unbuttoning his shirt and then slid the crisp cotton from his shoulders, revelling in the feel of his skin, so hot and satiny, under her fingers. She pressed a kiss to his collarbone, needing to feel that hot, smooth skin under her lips. Leo let out a groan as she touched her tongue to his skin, tasted salt.

'You will undo me before we've even begun...'

She looked up, mischief in her eyes. 'Would that be a bad thing?'

'A very bad thing—because I want to savour every moment.'

Smiling, he undid the tie on her jersey wrap dress and it fell open. Margo felt only a little self-conscious in her bra and pants, with the swell of her bump visible and making her shape so different from the last time they'd been together like this.

Yet they'd *never*, she realised, been together like this. So intimate. So tender. So honest.

Leo slid the dress off her shoulders and then rested one hand on her bump, his skin warm on hers. 'You are so very beautiful.'

'Even pregnant?'

'Especially pregnant. Knowing you are carrying my child makes you impossible to resist.'

He bent down and pressed a kiss to her bump, and then gently he laid her back on the rug, its soft bristles tickling her bare back as he stretched out beside her.

Margo gazed up at him, everything about her open and trusting as Leo pressed a kiss to her mouth and then worked his way lower, kissing her breasts and her bump, and then all the way down to her thighs. Margo gasped as he kissed her *there*, spreading her legs wide so he could have greater access, making her feel even more vulnerable…

And yet she didn't mind. She felt treasured rather than exposed, and she wanted Leo to feel the same way.

'My turn now,' she said with a little grin, and Leo arched an eyebrow as she pushed him onto his back.

'If you insist,' he said—and then let out a groan as Margo began to kiss him, taking her time, savouring the salty tang of his skin.

She kissed her way down his chest and Leo's hands tangled in her hair as she moved lower, his breath coming out in a hiss as she freed his arousal from his boxer shorts, sliding one hand up its smooth, hot length before taking it into her mouth.

'*Margo…*' His breath ended on a cry as his hips arched upwards.

Margo watched him with hot eyes, his own desire making hers ratchet higher.

Then Leo reached for her, pulling her up towards him

so she was straddling his hips. She sank onto his shaft with a sigh of relief that turned into a moan of pleasure as he began to move, his hands tightly gripping her hips so she moved with him in an exquisite rhythm.

The firelight cast shadows over their bodies as they moved together, climbing higher and higher towards that barely attainable peak. Logs shifted and cracked, sparks scattered, and Margo cried out as she finally reached the apex, drawing Leo even more tightly into her body as she threw her head back and her climax shuddered through her.

Afterwards they lay tangled together on the rug, warm and sated, their breathing only just starting to slow.

'Thank goodness Maria didn't come down for a glass of warm milk…' Leo said.

Margo stiffened. 'She wouldn't—?'

'She is known to on occasion. It helps her sleep.' He kissed the top of her head. 'But don't worry. No one came. Except you, that is.'

She laughed softly and snuggled up against him. 'And you.'

'Most certainly. And *that*, I have to say, was a long time to wait.'

'There wasn't…?' She hesitated, not wanting to spoil the mood but needing to know. 'There wasn't anyone else? Since…?'

'No one,' Leo told her firmly. 'No one but you for over two years now, Margo.'

'And there was no one but you for me, Leo. You *do* believe me?'

'Yes.'

He spoke with such certainty that she relaxed once more into his embrace. Just asking the question had made her tense.

They lay there in a comfortable silence, as the sweat cooled on their bodies and the fire cast its shadows, and Margo felt completely, wonderfully content. This, she thought, was what a true, loving marriage could and should be. If only it could last…

CHAPTER FOURTEEN

A FEW DAYS after Christmas Antonios and Lindsay came to the villa, all the way from New York. Margo had spent hours getting ready: supervising the preparations for meals, tweaking the decorations, and finally seeing to her outfit. She was nervous about meeting Leo's brother and his wife—both for her sake and his.

Their relationship had been growing stronger in the last few days, but it still felt fragile. They hadn't said those three important words, and Margo quaked inwardly to think of actually committing herself in that way to Leo, of making her frail hopes real and spoken. Of losing it all.

She'd known the worst to happen so many times; she couldn't help but expect it now.

With Antonios's upcoming arrival, Leo had withdrawn a bit, spending more time in the office, coming to bed late at night. At least they now shared a bed. They hadn't discussed it; Leo had simply joined Margo there on Christmas Eve, after they'd made love. And he'd continued to join her every night, much to her relief and joy.

The night before she'd turned to him, smoothed a thumb over the furrow in his forehead. 'Tell me what's going on,' she'd said quietly.

Leo had twitched under her caress. 'Nothing's going on.'

'Are you worried about seeing Antonios again?'

'I'm not worried.'

'But there's something. You haven't been yourself, Leo—'

'I'm fine.'

He'd rolled onto his side, away from her, and Margo had sunk back against the pillows, more hurt than she'd wanted to admit even to herself.

'Leave it alone,' he'd muttered, and they'd gone to sleep in silence.

Now she stood on the portico, shivering slightly in the wintry breeze, as Antonios and Lindsay's hired car came up the estate's sweeping drive. Leo joined her on the step, his expression inscrutable as the car came to a stop in front of them.

Margo had felt a distance between them this morning; apparently their new relationship didn't extend to the kind of honesty and intimacy she'd been looking for last night. Lesson learned.

Lindsay got out first, waving her welcome. She was beautiful in a pale, almost ethereal way, and she smiled at Margo. Leo had told her a few days ago that Lindsay suffered from social anxiety, but with Antonios's help was able to manage it. Margo wanted to make things as easy for her new sister-in-law as possible and she started forward, smiling her own welcome.

'I'm so very glad to meet you.'

'And I you. Although I haven't heard that much about you.' Lindsay gave Leo a teasing look, and he smiled back tightly.

Margo knew Lindsay had no idea about their complicated history; she certainly wasn't going to mention it now—not when she was wondering yet again just what *was* between her and Leo.

'Come inside,' she said, drawing Lindsay up the steps towards the villa. 'It's freezing out.'

Although Antonios was only just getting out of the car Margo could still feel the tension emanating from both of the brothers. Better, she decided, for them to have their reunion in private. Leo had already shown her he didn't want her involved.

Lindsay came behind her into the villa, stopping to admire the garlands of greenery looped over the banisters and along the doorways. 'Oh, but it's beautiful! Did *you* do this?'

'Yes, I wanted a proper Christmas,' Margo said, feeling rather shy.

Lindsay beamed at her. 'I love it. I wish I could make our apartment back in New York look half as nice. I'm hopeless with decorating and things like that. Hopeless with almost everything except for numbers.'

'I doubt that.'

Leo had told her that Lindsay was a brilliant mathematician, and was currently teaching at a university in New York City. Looking at her sister-in-law, Margo couldn't help but feel a bit intimidated. Lindsay might have social anxiety, but she hid it remarkably well. Margo was the one who felt and no doubt *looked* anxious…about so many things.

Xanthe, Ava and Parthenope came into the room, greeting Lindsay with warm hugs, reminding Margo that she was still on a somewhat fragile footing with Leo's sisters. It would come right in time, she told herself, and sat down on a settee while Maria came in with coffee for everyone. Just as things would with Leo. She had to trust that—had to believe that things would work out this time.

But that was easier said than done.

Eventually the three women finished their greetings and catch-up and turned to Margo.

'Leo is a dark horse,' Lindsay said teasingly. 'I didn't even know he was seeing someone.'

Margo's insides tensed. 'He likes to keep things quiet, I suppose,' she said.

'You're one to talk, Lindsay,' Xanthe said, grinning. 'Antonios showed up with *you* with no warning whatsoever!'

'That's true,' Lindsay agreed with a laugh.

Desperate to direct the spotlight away from herself, Margo said, 'That sounds like there's a story to be told.'

Lindsay agreed, and then told Margo how she and Antonios had met and married in New York City all within a week.

'When you know, you know, right?' she said, with a smile that Margo suspected was meant to create solidarity but only made everything inside her shrink with apprehension.

Lindsay made it sound as if everything was obvious and easy when you were in love, but Margo still felt so much uncertainty, so much fear. She wanted to embrace this new life, and yet still she was holding back, and Leo was too. Perhaps they always would.

It was certainly hard for *her*. Everyone had let her down at one point or another. No one had been there for her when she'd needed it. It was so difficult to let go of that history—not to make it affect her choices even now. Difficult not to brace herself for when Leo would fail her, or say he'd had enough, or just walk away. Everyone else had—why wouldn't he?

Antonios and Leo finally came into the sitting room. Margo shot Leo a swift, searching look, but she couldn't tell anything from his face and she wondered what had passed between the two brothers.

The conversation moved on to Parthenope's family, and little Timon's antics. Margo sat back and let it all wash over her; it felt good to be part of a family—even if she was just sitting and listening to everyone else. She caught Leo's eye and he smiled at her, and the uncertainty that had been knotting her stomach eased a little.

It was going to be okay. She would believe that. At least she would try.

Leo sat on the settee across from Margo, barely listening to everyone's chatter. The stilted conversation he'd had with Antonios out on the steps replayed in his mind.

It had been strange and unsettling to see his brother again, standing there in front of their childhood home, remembering the death of both of their parents, a decade of hostility and suspicion between them… Leo had felt himself tense, his hands ball into instinctive fists. He'd seen from the set of Antonios's jaw and his narrowed eyes that he felt the same.

They could clear the air, they could forgive the past, they could say they were moving on, but the reality was that memories still clung. They still held power. And if he couldn't move past things with Antonios, how could he with Margo?

He wanted to tell her he loved her, wanted to trust that what they had was real and lasting. But the memory of her last rejection still had the power to hurt. To make him stay silent. They'd had just over a month together…a few intense moments. Nothing, he acknowledged, that actually constituted a real, loving, trusting relationship.

'How's marriage?' Antonios had asked as they'd stood outside in wintry silence.

'Fine.'

'I didn't know you were seeing anyone.'

'It's not as if we keep each other up to date on our personal lives,' Leo had answered. He'd meant to sound light, but it had come out terse and dismissive instead. 'You're one to talk, anyway,' he'd added, trying for a joke, but it had fallen flat.

Antonios had just nodded, his jaw bunched, and they hadn't spoken again until they were settled in the sitting room with everyone else—and then only about innocuous matters.

Leo's gaze kept straying to Margo. She was listening to everyone, but he thought she looked tense, maybe even unhappy, and he wished they could be alone. Wished he could be sure of her feelings…and of his own.

'Is everything all right between you and Antonios?' Margo asked as they got ready for bed that evening.

They hadn't spoken much during the day, busy as they'd both been with their guests. Margo, Leo noticed now, looked pale and tired, with lines of strain around her eyes.

'As well as they can be, I suppose,' he said as he stretched out on the bed.

Leo still kept his clothes in the adjoining room, but he'd brought a few things into Margo's bedroom: his books, his reading glasses, his pyjamas. Small yet intimate things that spoke of building a life together. But lying there he felt as if his presence in Margo's life, in her bed, was transient.

Margo took down her hair, and Leo felt a frisson of sensual pleasure as he watched her raise her slender arms, anticipating the sudden tumble of dark, wavy hair down to her waist.

'What does that mean?' she asked as she reached for the satin nightdress she wore to bed and quickly undressed.

Leo had tantalising glimpses of her breasts and thighs, milky-pale and soft-looking, before she shrugged the nightdress on and slid under the covers, pillows propped behind her as she looked at him and waited for his answer.

'We have ten years of hard history,' Leo said slowly. 'Even though we've talked about it and tried to put it behind us, I don't think it's that easy or simple.'

'No,' Margo agreed quietly. 'It isn't.'

He knew she was thinking of her own past hurts. As much as she might want to, could she move on from her appalling childhood and the many wrongs that had been done to her? Could *they* move on from the hurt they'd caused each other?

He wasn't about to ask those questions. They spoke of his own past, his own uncertainty and fear. He'd spent his childhood trying to prove himself to his father—wanting Evangelos to love him,and receiving only rejection.

And it was those experiences that kept him silent now.

'Do you think things will get better in time?' Margo asked, her gaze serious and intent on him.

For a second Leo thought she was asking about things with them. Then he realised she meant Antonios.

'Maybe,' he said with a shrug.

He didn't sound hopeful.

Wanting to end the discussion, he reached for her, wrapping a thick tendril of hair around his wrist as he pulled her gently towards him. She came with a smile, her features softened and suffused with desire, their bodies bumping up against one another as Leo brushed a kiss across her mouth.

They'd made love many times in the days since Christmas Eve. Their chemistry had always been explosive, right from the beginning, but in the last week it had become even more intimate and arousing.

Margo let out a soft little sigh as she brought her arms up around his neck, her body yielding to his in a way that made Leo's head spin and desire spiral dizzily inside him. He slid his hand from her shoulder to her waist to her hip, loving the silky feel of her skin, the ripe fullness of her breasts and hips.

She twitched slightly beneath his caress and he stilled his hand. 'What is it?'

'Just the normal fears of a pregnant woman,' she said with an uncertain little laugh. 'I feel fat.'

'Fat? *Fat?* Margo, you are not remotely fat. You are fecund and beautiful and glowing. I like your body more, I think, than before you were carrying our baby.'

'You do *not*!'

'You doubt me?' he said in a mock growl, and she let out another laugh, this one breathless with anticipation.

'I do.'

'Then perhaps I should prove to you just how beautiful you are,' Leo said, and bent his head to her breasts, taking his time to give each one his full, lascivious attention.

Margo let out a sigh of pleasure, her hands tangling in his hair, and Leo lifted his head.

'Does that satisfy you?' he demanded, and she gazed at him with a mischievous smile.

'Not…quite.'

'I see I'll have to prove it to you some more.'

'You just might.'

Laughing softly, he slid a hand between her thighs. 'I can do a lot of proving,' he murmured, 'if that's your wish.'

'It is,' Margo whispered back, her hips arching upwards. And then they lost themselves to their shared pleasure.

The next day Leo and Antonios repaired to the office, to discuss matters relating to Marakaios Enterprises, and Lindsay sought out Margo up in the soon-to-be nursery, where she was comparing fabric swatches.

'Hello,' she said, poking her head around the door, and Margo gave a self-conscious smile before welcoming her in.

'Sorry, I'm not trying to hide away.' She rubbed her lower back while motioning to the swatches. 'Just trying to make a decision about fabric. It can take ages for it to come in once you place an order.'

'I wouldn't know,' Lindsay answered with a laugh. 'But Leo mentioned you worked in decorating before…?'

'I was a buyer for a department store in Paris. Home furnishings.' It occurred to her this must seem like a rather useless job to a brilliant mathematician, but Lindsay appeared genuinely interested.

'Do you miss it? When Antonios and I lived here I missed my old life a lot more than I thought I would. My old job…'

Margo was intrigued to think that Lindsay and Antonios's marriage hadn't always been as perfect as it now seemed.

'I don't *miss* it exactly,' she answered slowly. 'But I miss feeling productive and useful sometimes.'

Lindsay nodded in sympathy before saying in a rush, 'Look, I think I may have put my foot in it yesterday, which isn't all that surprising, considering how bad I am at social situations. But when I mentioned not knowing that you and Leo were dating…' She swallowed, a blush staining her pale cheeks. 'Well, it's none of my business whether you were dating or not. I didn't mean to make you feel awkward.'

'But you noticed that you *did*?' Margo answered with an uncertain laugh.

'I'm sorry.'

'No, don't be. It was a perfectly innocent question. And the truth is my relationship with Leo is…complicated.'

'I can relate to that.'

'Can you?' Margo glanced at her sister-in-law with open curiosity. 'Because from where I'm standing you and Antonios seem to have the fairytale.'

'Oh, don't say that!' Lindsay cried, and Margo raised her eyebrows. 'It used to seem like a fairytale,' she explained. 'Meeting the way we did in New York. Antonios sweeping me straight off my feet.' Lindsay sighed and shook her head. 'But life isn't a fairytale, you know? Reality sets in. And when it did for Antonios and me, it was hard.'

'How so?'

'Did Leo tell you about my social anxiety?'

'A bit…'

'As soon as we were married Antonios whisked me off here and put me in charge of the household. He thought he was honouring me, but in truth it just terrified me. I've had social anxiety since I was a child—talking in front of crowds, being the centre of attention…it all makes me start to panic. And when I landed here…with all of Antonios's sisters as well as his mother looking at me, measuring me…it was hard.'

'But his sisters love you now,' Margo remarked.

Lindsay smiled wryly. 'That doesn't mean they weren't taken aback when Antonios showed up with me out of the blue.'

'The same way Leo showed up with me,' Margo admitted with a laugh. 'Poor girls. They've had an awful lot of shocks.'

'So why *did* you and Leo marry, if you don't mind me asking? *Were* you dating…?' Lindsay's blush deepened. 'Sorry, I'm being inexcusably nosy. But, if you don't mind me saying so, you remind me a little bit of me when I came here. A little overwhelmed…a little lost.'

'Do I?' Margo could hear how stiff and stilted her voice

sounded and busied herself organising the swatches of fabric, just to give herself a little time to order her thoughts.

'Am I wrong?' Lindsay asked quietly.

'Not exactly. Coming here as Leo's wife was overwhelming—especially considering the circumstances.' She glanced down at her bump and Lindsay nodded her understanding. 'I don't have a lot of experience with big families or houses. I've pretty much been on my own my whole life.'

'As have I,' Lindsay said quietly.

Margo looked at her in surprise. 'We seem to have quite a bit in common.'

'Not least being married to difficult Marakaios men.'

They both laughed at that, and then Margo said seriously, 'But Antonios seems to dote on you.'

'Antonios can be stubborn and set in his ways. He tends not to see another person's perspective unless it's pointed out to him. *Repeatedly.*' Lindsay softened this observation with a smile and added, 'But I'm utterly in love with him, and he with me, and that makes all the difference.'

'Yes, I'm sure it does,' Margo murmured.

She thought of how she and Leo had made love last night, spending the whole night sleeping in each other's arms. Was that love? It seemed like it, on the surface, but the fact remained that she still felt wary and guarded, and she thought Leo did too. They were both still holding back, both afraid to commit fully to their marriage… Or maybe Leo just didn't want to. Maybe what they had was enough—was all he wanted.

And yet she knew she wanted more. She wanted the fairytale.

CHAPTER FIFTEEN

A MONTH PASSED in wintry days spent with Margo decorating the nursery and managing the household, getting to know Leo's sisters—and getting to know Leo.

They spent far more time together now than they ever had in their two years of dirty weekends and meals out. They chatted about everything—from politics to music and books, to places they'd like to visit. He was becoming as good a friend as he was a lover.

And yet she still felt that reticence in him, and in herself. They still hadn't said *I love you*, hadn't discussed anything about the future. Leo still hadn't moved his things into her bedroom.

As the weeks passed Margo wondered if this wasn't actually a *good* thing. If Leo kept a little distance, then she could too. Maybe they could enjoy each other's company and bodies and still stay safe. Still not risk getting hurt.

Yet she knew that for a lie when she thought about the possibility of losing Leo. She would be utterly devastated.

At the end of January Leo came into the house, where she'd been browsing through a catalogue of baby toys, and asked if she'd come to the office with him.

'The office? Why?'

'I need your opinion on something.'

Surprised and a bit bemused, she walked with him across the estate to the long, low-lying building that overlooked the olive groves.

'What do you think of these?' he asked, and gestured to a box of olive-based bath supplies.

Frowning a little, Margo examined the items, noting the pleasingly thick glass bottles, the nutty smell of the olives.

'They feel expensive,' she offered. 'Although they smell a bit more like cooking oil than something you'd want to put in your bath.'

He nodded. 'I was afraid of that. I want to develop a new range of bath products to supply the Adair chain of hotels, but I don't think these are up to scratch.'

'A little olive oil goes a long way, I suppose,' Margo answered with a smile.

'I could use your expertise here,' Leo said. 'If you're willing to give it. Someone with a good eye for design and good taste to offer an opinion about our merchandise.'

Margo just stared.

'Not a full-time job, necessarily,' he continued. 'I know with the baby coming you wouldn't want that. But you have a lot of talent and expertise to offer, Margo, and I don't want to squander it.'

And so she started going into the office two days a week—to review the different products Marakaios Enterprises was offering and strategise the best way to market them. She enjoyed the work—and even more so because it meant she and Leo were working together…a true partnership.

Leo glanced across the breakfast table and smiled to see Margo balancing her teacup on top of her bump. Her hair was loose and dark about her face, her expression thoughtful as she read a journal about decorative art. They'd been married for only two months but they were already acting like an old married couple, reading their separate periodicals over breakfast.

Not that Leo minded. He loved these mornings with Margo, even when they weren't talking to each other. Just being in her presence, seeing her smile or watching the way her eyes darkened intently as she listened to him, made him happy.

Several weeks ago Margo had asked him if he was happy and Leo hadn't been able to answer. Now he knew he could. Yes, he was happy with Margo. He was happy—and in love—with his wife.

Just acknowledging that fact to himself gave him a little fizz of anticipation, as well as a twist of apprehension. He wanted to tell her how he felt, *all* he felt, and yet he held back. No time felt right. What if she told him she didn't love him back? What if she wasn't capable of it? He understood why she'd kept herself from love and life before, but it wouldn't make it any easier to accept now.

Rejection, Leo thought bleakly, was still rejection.

'How would you like to go to Paris?' he asked now, and she looked up from her journal, her eyes widening in surprise.

'Paris? Why?'

'I have a little business there. We could make it pleasure too, though. We could check on your apartment and see the city together. Visit some of our old haunts.'

'That sounds good,' Margo said slowly, almost as if she didn't trust that he'd want to go to Paris with her. 'It would be great to check in with Achat too. I gave my notice, obviously, but it would be good to have a proper goodbye. I worked there a long time.'

'Very well. Shall I make the arrangements? We could leave tomorrow.'

Margo nodded, her gaze still moving over him, and Leo looked away. He didn't want anything in his face to reveal the surprise he was planning for her.

They left early the next morning, driving to Athens and then flying on to Paris; they were in Margo's apartment on the Île de la Cité by mid-afternoon.

Leo stood on the threshold of the living room and gazed at the picture window overlooking Paris, the twin towers of Notre-Dame visible in the distance.

He'd asked Margo to marry him here. He'd felt the painful sting of rejection, the bitter and furious hurt that had led to the baby boy now nestled inside her waiting to be born. So much had changed, and yet for a moment he felt mired by the past.

He didn't actually know what Margo wanted. Once, six months ago, he'd thought he did. He'd asked her to marry him, feeling confident of her answer.

Looking back, he knew that his confidence had in fact been arrogance. Margo had given him no hint that she'd wanted a ring on her finger. Everything about her—her bold, sassy, sensual confidence, her easy acceptance of their arrangement—had indicated otherwise. And yet she'd admitted that the persona she'd adopted was nothing more than a mask.

So did the *real* Margo, the lovely, thoughtful, interesting woman he'd come to know beneath that mask, want what he wanted now?

'Leo…' She came up behind him and rested her hands lightly on his shoulders.

Leo blinked back the memories before turning around to face her and slip his arms around her waist.

'We'll always have Paris,' he quipped, and though she smiled he saw her eyes were troubled.

'Will we?' she asked softly, sadly, and too late Leo realised how that had sounded.

They would always have Paris and the memories they'd made here...whether they wanted them or not.

Margo tried to banish the disquiet that fluttered through as she saw Leo's eyebrows draw together in a faint frown. She'd been nervous about coming back to Paris, to the city where they'd met so often during their affair, and the very room where Margo had rejected him. She didn't think she'd imagined the suddenly shuttered look on Leo's face as he'd come into her apartment, and she had a terrible feeling he was remembering how he'd proposed to her here and what her answer had been.

Now, however, he smiled, his face clearing, and looked around her sitting room. 'Do you know, before I came here I would have thought you'd have some modern, sleek penthouse? All chrome and leather and modern art.'

'You mean like your bachelor pad in Athens? I prefer a homier place to live.'

'Which is why you were a buyer of home furnishings, I suppose?'

She nodded and he strolled around the apartment, noting the squashy velveteen sofa, the Impressionist prints, the porcelain ornaments and figurines. She'd had a lot of her things sent to Greece, but there were certainly enough left for Leo to examine and make her feel oddly exposed.

'How did you get into the buying business, anyway?' he asked as he picked up a carved wooden figurine of a mother holding her infant.

It had been whittled from one piece of wood and the result was a sinuous, fluid sculpture in which it was impossible to tell where the mother finished and the child began. Margo had always loved it, but never had it seemed so revealing of her life, her secret desires and heartache.

'I got a job with Achat, working on a sales counter, when I was sixteen. From there I moved up through the ranks,' she said. 'I've never actually worked anywhere else.'

'And you wanted to go into the buying side of things? Home furnishings in particular?'

'Yes, that was what I always liked.'

The bedsits and sheltered housing, the homeless shelters and foster placements that had comprised her childhood homes had never felt like proper places to grow up. Safe or loving places. And she had, Margo knew, been trying to create that for herself—through her job and in her own apartment.

Somehow she had a feeling Leo knew that too.

He put the figurine down and turned to her. 'You have a beautiful home here,' he said. 'You have a real talent for making a space feel cosy and welcoming.'

'Thank you.'

'If there are any more things you'd like to take to Greece I can arrange for them to be shipped.'

'I'll look around tomorrow and box things up.'

He smiled and reached for her again. Margo snuggled into him, grateful for the feel of his arms around her, making her feel safe. *For now.*

While Margo went to Achat to say her goodbyes Leo attended to his business in the city. He'd been acting a bit mysteriously, which had made Margo wonder what he was doing or planning, but she told herself not to be nervous and just to wait and see.

In any case, her arrival at Achat put Leo out of her mind for a little while, as she was caught up in reunions with different acquaintances, a bittersweet meeting with her boss, who wished she could stay, and then a catch-up with Sophie.

They left the office for a café with deep velvet chairs and spindly little tables a few blocks from Achat. Sophie ordered them both bowl-sized cups of hot chocolate with lashings of whipped cream.

'A celebration,' she proclaimed, 'since things seem to have turned out all right for you.'

'How do you know they have?' Margo challenged as she took a sip of the deliciously rich hot chocolate.

'You haven't sent me any panicked texts,' Sophie answered, 'and, more importantly, you look *happy*, Margo. Happier than I think I've ever seen you.'

'I *am* happy…' Margo said quietly.

Sophie arched an eyebrow. 'Why do you sound so uncertain, then?'

'Because happiness can be so fleeting.' She took a deep breath. 'And Leo hasn't actually told me he loves me.'

'Have you told *him*?'

'No…'

'Well, then.'

When Margo had first been pregnant Sophie had heard the full story of Leo's proposal and Margo's rejection.

'Can you really blame him for not going first?' she asked, and Margo sighed.

'Not really.'

'So why *haven't* you told him you love him?'

'Because I'm afraid that's not what he wants to hear. Because we're both holding back.'

'Then stop,' Sophie suggested with a smile.

'It's not that simple,' Margo said. 'It's…' She hesitated, thoughts and fears swirling around in her mind. 'I feel like if I try for too much—if I do anything to jeopardise what we have—it will all topple like a child's tower of bricks because it's not strong enough to stand...'

'Stand what?' Sophie asked gently.

'*Anything*. Anything bad.' Margo swallowed. 'I know I'm afraid, and that I'm letting my fear control my actions. I understand that, Sophie, trust me.'

'But it's keeping you from doing something about it.'

'I think I'd rather just hold on to what we have and be happy with it than try for more and lose,' Margo confessed quietly. 'If that makes me a coward, so be it.'

Sophie eyed her sceptically. 'As long as you *are* happy,' she said after a moment.

Margo didn't answer.

Sophie's words still pinged around in her head as she headed back to her apartment. *Was* she happy? *Could* this be enough?

Maybe Sophie was right, and Leo was holding back simply because *she* was. Maybe if she made the first move and told him she loved him he would tell her back.

They were going out to dinner tonight. Leo had made the arrangements, although he hadn't told Margo where. But they'd be alone, and it might even be romantic, and it would be a perfect opportunity for Margo to tell Leo the truth.

To tell him she loved him.

She spent a long time getting ready that evening. First she had a long soak in the tub, and then she did her nails, hair and make-up before donning a new maternity dress of soft black jersey.

It had a daring V-neck that made the most of her pregnancy-enhanced assets and draped lovingly over her bump before swirling about her knees. She'd put her hair up for the simple pleasure of being able to take it down again in

Leo's presence later that night, and had slipped her feet into her favourite pair of black suede stiletto heels.

And now she waited—because Leo still wasn't home.

He'd been due back at seven to collect Margo for their date, but as the minutes ticked by Margo's unease grew. It figured that the one night she'd decided to tell Leo how she felt he'd be AWOL. It almost seemed like a sign, a portent of things to come. Or rather not to come.

At seven forty-five she texted Leo. At eight she took off her heels and her earrings—both had been starting to hurt—and curled up on her bed.

Her phone rang at eight-fifteen.

'Margo, I'm so sorry—'

'What happened?' Her voice was quiet and yet filled with hurt.

'I had a meeting with Adair Hotels. It's an important deal and the meeting ran long. I didn't even realise the time…'

'It's okay,' she said. And it *was* okay. At least it should have been okay. It would have been okay if she hadn't built this evening up in her own mind.

Maybe she'd built *everything* up in her own mind.

In that moment she felt as if she couldn't trust anything or anyone, least of all herself. It was nothing more than a missed dinner, and yet it was so much more. It was everything.

'When will you be back?' she asked, and Leo sighed.

'I don't know. Late. Talks are still ongoing, and we'll most likely go out for drinks afterwards.' He hesitated and then said, 'Don't wait up.'

And somehow that stung too.

She was being ridiculous, over-emotional, overreacting. She knew that. And yet she still hung up on Leo without replying.

* * *

Leo stared at the phone, the beep of Margo disconnecting the call still echoing through his ear. Had she actually just hung up on him? Simply because he'd missed dinner?

He let out a long sigh and tossed his phone on the desk. He felt as if something big had happened, something momentous, and damned if he knew what it was.

But then he hadn't known what was going on for a while. For the last month he and Margo had been existing in an emotional stasis which he suspected suited them both fine. Neither of them had been ready to take their relationship up to that next level. To say they loved each other… to bare the truth of their hearts.

At least *he* hadn't. Maybe Margo had nothing to say… nothing to bare.

'Leo?' One of his staff poked his head through the doorway, eyebrows raised. 'Are you ready?'

Leo nodded. This deal was too important for him to become distracted about Margo.

And yet as he went back into the conference room he couldn't stop thinking about her. About the hurt he'd heard in her voice and the way she'd hung up on him. About all the painful truths she'd shared about her childhood and all the things he hadn't said.

He lasted an hour before he called the meeting to a halt.

'I'm sorry, gentlemen, but we can resume tomorrow. I need to get home to my wife.'

After she'd hung up on Leo, Margo peeled off her dress and ran a bath. Perhaps a nice long soak in the tub would help alleviate her misery—or at least give her a little perspective. It was one missed dinner…one little argument. It didn't have to mean anything.

Sighing, Margo slipped into the water and closed her

eyes. She felt as if she couldn't shift the misery that had taken up residence in her chest, as if a stone were pressing down on her.

At first Margo thought the pain in her belly was simply the weight of that disappointment and heartache, but then the twinges intensified and she realised she was feeling actual physical pain. Something was wrong.

She pressed her hands to her bump, realising she hadn't felt a kick in a while—a few hours at least. She'd become used to feeling those lovely flutters. Now she felt another knifing pain through her stomach, and then a sudden gush of fluid, and she watched in dawning shock and horror as the water around her bloomed red.

CHAPTER SIXTEEN

THE APARTMENT WAS quiet and empty when Leo came into the foyer just after nine o'clock.

'Margo?'

He tossed his keys on the table, a sudden panic icing inside him. Had she left? Left *him*? He realised in that moment that he'd been bracing himself for such a thing, perhaps from the moment they'd married. Waiting for another rejection.

'Margo?' he called again, but the only answer was the ringing silence that seemed to reverberate through the empty rooms of the apartment.

He poked his head through the doorway of her bedroom, and saw how the lamplight cast a golden pool onto the empty bed. Her dress and shoes were discarded and crumpled on the floor and the bathroom door was ajar, light spilling from within. All was silent.

He was about to turn back when he heard a sound from the bathroom—the slosh of water. He froze for a millisecond, and then in three strides crossed to the bathroom, threw open the door, and saw Margo lying in a tub full of rose-tinted water, her head lolling back, her face drained of colour.

'Margo—' Her name was a cry, a plea, a prayer. Leo

fumbled for his phone even as he reached for her, drew her out of the tub. 'Margo…' he whispered.

She glanced up at him, her face with a waxy sheen, her eyes luminous.

'I've lost the baby, haven't I?'

'I don't know—' He stopped, for she'd slumped in his arms, unconscious.

Margo came to, lying on a stretcher. Two paramedics were wheeling her to an ambulance, and panic clutched at her so hard she could barely speak.

'My baby—'

One of them reassured her that they were taking her to a hospital, and Leo reached for her hand. His hand felt cold, as cold as hers. He was scared, she realised. He knew the worst was happening.

The worst *always* happened.

Just hours ago she'd been buoying up her courage to tell Leo she loved him. Now everything had fallen apart. Nothing could be the same. Her relationship with Leo had been expedient at its core; without this child kicking in her womb there was no need for a marriage.

And yet she couldn't think about losing Leo on top of losing the baby; it was too much to bear. So she forced her mind to go blank, and after a few seconds her panic was replaced by a numb, frozen feeling—a feeling she'd thought she'd never have to experience again.

It was the way she'd felt when she'd realised Annelise was gone. It was the only way she'd known how to cope. And yet she hadn't coped at all. And she didn't think she could cope now—except by remaining frozen. Numb.

She felt distant from the whole scene—as if she were floating above the ambulance, watching as the paramedics sat next to her, taking her vitals.

'Blood pressure is dropping steadily.'

She barely felt a flicker of anything as they searched for the baby's heartbeat. They found it, but from the paramedics' mutterings it was clearly weak.

'Baby appears to be in distress.'

In distress. It seemed such a little term for so terrible a moment.

'Margo…Margo.' Leo was holding her hand, his face close to hers. 'It's going to be okay. *Agapi mou*, I promise—'

My love. The words didn't move her now, didn't matter at all. 'You can't promise anything,' she said, and turned her face away.

The next few minutes passed in a blur as the ambulance arrived, siren wailing, at a hospital on the other side of the Île de la Cité—one of Paris's oldest hospitals, a beautiful building Margo had walked by many times but never been inside.

Now she was rushed into a room on the emergency ward, and doctors surrounded her as they took her vitals yet again. She could see Leo standing outside, demanding to be allowed in. A doctor was arguing with him.

Margo felt herself sliding into unconsciousness, one hand cradling her bump—the only connection she had to the baby she was afraid she'd never meet.

'Madame Marakaios?'

A doctor touched her arm, bringing her back to wakefulness.

'You have had a placental abruption. Do you know what that is?'

'Is my baby dying?' Margo asked. Her voice sounded slurred.

'We need to perform an emergency Caesarean section as your baby is in distress. Do you give your consent?'

'But I'm only twenty-seven weeks…'

'It is your child's only chance, *madame*,' the doctor said, and wordlessly Margo nodded.

What else could she do?

They began to prep her for surgery and Margo lay there, tears silently snaking down her face; it appeared she wasn't that frozen after all.

And yet neither was she surprised. Wasn't this what happened? You let people in, you loved them, and they left you. Her baby. *Leo.*

The last thought Margo had as she was put under anaesthetic was that maybe it would have been better not to have trusted or loved at all.

CHAPTER SEVENTEEN

Leo paced the waiting room restlessly, his hands bunched into fists. He hadn't been allowed inside the operating room and he felt furious and helpless and desperately afraid. He couldn't lose their son. He couldn't lose Margo.

He wished more than ever that he'd had the courage to tell her he loved her. Three little words and yet he'd held back. He'd held back in so many ways, not wanting to risk rejection or hurt, and all he could do now was call himself a fool. A frightened fool for not speaking the truth of his heart to his wife.

If Margo made it through this, he vowed he would tell her. He would tell her everything he felt.

'Monsieur Marakaios?' A doctor still in his surgical scrubs came through the steel double doors.

Leo's jaw bunched and he sprang forward. 'You have news? Is my wife—?'

'Your wife and son are all right,' the man said quietly, 'although weak.'

'Weak—?'

'Your wife lost a great deal of blood. She is stable, but she will have a few weeks of recovery ahead of her.'

'And the baby? My son?' A lump formed in his throat as he waited for the doctor to respond.

'He's in the Neonatal Intensive Care Unit,' the doctor

answered. 'He's very small, and his lungs aren't mature. He'll need to stay in hospital for some weeks at least.'

Leo nodded jerkily; he didn't trust himself to speak for a moment. When he had his emotions under control, he managed, 'Please—I'd like to see my wife.'

Margo had been moved to a private room on the ward, and was lying in bed, her eyes closed.

'Margo?' he said softly, and touched her hand.

She opened her eyes and stared at him for a long moment, and then she turned her head away from him.

Leo felt tears sting his eyes. 'Margo, it's okay. You're all right and our son is all right.'

'He's alive, you mean,' she said flatly.

Leo blinked. 'Yes, alive. Small, and his lungs aren't mature, but he's stable—'

'You can't know that.'

'The doctor just said—'

She shook her head.

Leo frowned and touched her hand. 'Margo, it's going to be okay.'

She withdrew her hand from his. 'Stop making promises you can't keep, Leo.'

Helplessly Leo stared at her, not knowing what to say or do. 'I know it's been frightening—'

'You don't know *anything*!' She cut across him, her voice choking on a sob. 'You don't know what it's like to lose everything again.'

'But you didn't—we didn't—'

'I want you to go.' She closed her eyes, tears leaking from under her lids and making silvery tracks down her cheeks. 'Please—please go.'

It went against every instinct he had to leave Margo alone in this moment. He wanted to tell her how he loved her, and yet she couldn't even bear to look at him. How had this happened?

'Margo—' he began, only to realise from the way her breathing had evened out that she was asleep. He touched her cheek, wanting her to know even in sleep how he felt, and then quietly left the room.

'It's difficult to say what's going to happen,' the doctor told Leo when he went to ask for more details about his son's condition. 'Of course there have been terrific strides made in the care of premature babies. But I don't like to give any promises at this stage, because premature infants' immune systems aren't fully developed and neither are their lungs. It's very easy for them to catch an infection and have it become serious.'

Leo nodded, his throat tight. He'd just tried to promise Margo it was going to be okay. But she was right: he couldn't promise anything. And he didn't know if their marriage, fragile as it was, would survive this.

He stood outside the neonatal ICU and watched his impossibly small son flail tiny red fists. He was covered in tubes to help him breathe, eat, live. It made Leo ache with a fierce love—and a desperate fear.

Eventually he went back to see Margo. She was awake and sitting up in bed, and while the sight of her lifted his spirits, the expression on her face did not.

'The doctor says the next few weeks will be crucial,' Leo said.

Margo nodded; she looked almost indifferent to this news.

'He'll have to stay in hospital for a while—at least a month.'

Another nod.

'He can't be taken out of the ICU,' Leo ventured, 'and

we can't hold him yet, but I could wheel you up there so you can at least see him?'

Margo stared at him for a moment before she answered quietly, 'I don't think so.'

Leo stared at her in shock. 'Margo—'

'I told you before, I'd like to be alone.'

She turned away from him and he stared at her helplessly.

'Margo, please. Tell me what's going on.'

'Nothing is going on. I've just realised.' She drew a quick, sharp breath. 'I can't do this. I thought I could—I wanted to—but I can't.'

'Can't do what?'

'This.' She gestured with one limp hand to the space between them. 'Marriage. Motherhood. Any of it. I can't let myself love someone and have them taken away again. I just...*can't*.'

'Margo, I won't leave you—'

'Maybe not physically,' she allowed. 'You have too much honour for that. But you told me yourself you didn't love me—'

'That was months ago—'

'And nothing's changed, has it?' She lifted her resolute gaze to his in weary challenge. 'Nothing's changed,' she repeated.

Leo wondered if she was saying that nothing had changed for *her*. She didn't love *him*.

For a second he remained silent, and a second was all Margo needed for affirmation.

She nodded. 'I thought so. We only had a couple of months together, Leo. They were lovely, I suppose, but that's all they were.'

'No.' Finally he found his voice, along with his resolve.

'*No*, Margo. I don't accept that. I won't let you torpedo our marriage simply because you're afraid.'

'Of *course* I'm afraid,' she snapped, her voice rising in anger. 'Do you even know what it's like to lose someone—?'

'I lost both my parents,' Leo answered. 'So, yes, I do.'

'Yes, of course you do,' she acknowledged. 'But a *child.* A child *I* was responsible for—a child who looked to *me* for love and care and food and everything—' Her voice broke and her shoulders began to shake with sobs.

'Margo…Margo…' Leo crooned softly and, sitting on the edge of the bed, gently put his arms around her.

She stilled, unable to move away from him but still trying to keep herself distant. Safe. But safety, Leo realised, was Margo knowing how he truly felt.

'I love you,' he said, and then, in case she still doubted him, he said it again. 'I love you. And that will never change. No matter what happens. *No matter what.*'

To his surprise and dismay her shoulders shook harder.

She pulled away from him, wiping the tears from her face. 'Oh, Leo. I don't deserve you.'

'*Deserve?* What does this have to do with deserving?'

'It's *my* fault Annelise died. Maybe it's my fault our son is in such danger. I might have done something… I don't deserve…'

'Margo, hush.' Tenderly he wiped the tears from her cheeks. 'You must stop blaming yourself for what happened.'

She'd been tortured by both guilt and grief for years, and he longed to release her.

'What happened to Annelise could have happened to any child, any mother. And you were only a child yourself. As for our son…you've been so careful during this pregnancy. I've seen you. Nothing is your fault.'

She shook her head but he continued.

'You must let the past go and forgive yourself. You must look to your future—*our* future—and our son's future. Because I love you, and I wish I'd told you before. I wish you'd known how much I loved you when you went into surgery. I wish you'd had that to hold on to.'

She blinked up at him, searching his face. 'Do you mean it, Leo?' she asked quietly. 'Do you really mean it?'

'With all my heart.'

'I haven't even said how I feel.'

'If you don't love me,' he answered steadily, 'it's all right. I can wait—'

'But I *do* love you.' She cut him off. 'I was going to tell you tonight, when we had dinner—'

'Nothing turned out quite as we expected, did it?' he said, and pressed a kiss to her palm. 'But now we've told each other, and we have our son, and I will do everything in my power to keep you safe and secure and—'

'I believe you!' With a trembling laugh she pressed the palm he'd just kissed against his lips. 'You don't have to convince me.'

'I want to spend a lifetime convincing you.'

Tears sparkled on her lashes. 'And our little boy…?'

'Why don't you come and see him?'

Margo's heart was beating with thuds so hard they made her feel sick as Leo wheeled her up to the ICU. He parked the wheelchair in front of the glass and Margo stared at the row of plastic cradles, the tubes and the wires, the tiny beings fighting so hard for life.

And then she saw the words *'Enfant Marakaios'* and everything in her clenched hard. Her son. Hers and Leo's.

'Oh, Leo,' she whispered, and reached for his hand.

They stared silently at the baby they'd made, now waving his fists angrily.

'He's got a lot of spirit—or so the doctor says,' Leo said shakily. 'He'll fight hard.'

Margo felt a hot rush of shame that she'd considered, even for a moment, protecting herself against the pain of loving this little boy. Of loving Leo. She'd spent a lifetime apart, atoning for her sins, trying to keep her shattered heart safe. But Leo, with his kindness and understanding and love, had put her back together again. Had made her want to try. To fight, and fight hard—just as their son was.

'I'm sorry—' she began, but Leo shook his head.

'No, don't be sorry. Just enjoy this moment. Enjoy our family.'

'Our little man,' Margo whispered, and then looked up at Leo.

He smiled down at her, his eyes bright with tears. Her family, Margo thought, right here.

There were no certainties—not for anyone. No guarantees of a happily-ever-after, no promises that life would flow smoothly. Life was a rough river, full of choppy currents, and the only thing she could do was grab on to those she loved and hold on. Hold on for ever.

And, clinging to Leo's hand, that was just what she was going to do.

EPILOGUE

'WHERE ARE WE GOING?' Margo asked as they stepped out onto the pavement in front of her apartment.

It was three months since their son had been born, and he was coming home from the hospital tomorrow. To celebrate, Leo was taking her out to dinner.

It had been a long, harrowing three months.

Annas—the name meant 'a gift given by God'—had had several lung infections that had terrified both Leo and Margo at the time, and twice it had been touch and go. Margo had felt more fear then than she ever had before, and yet with Leo's support and strength she'd met every challenge head-on, determined to believe in her son, to imbue him with all the strength and love she felt.

And he was healthy now—weighing just over five pounds, and more precious to Leo and Margo than they ever could have known.

Leo hailed a cab, and as the car pulled to the kerb he leaned over the window to give directions. He'd been making a big secret of their destination, which made Margo smile.

When the cab pulled up to the Eiffel Tower she looked at him in surprise. 'Sightseeing…?'

'In a way,' he answered, and drew her by the hand from

the cab to the base of the tower, where a man stood by the elevator that surged up its centre, waiting for them.

'*Bon soir*, Monsieur Marakios,' he said as he ushered them into the lift.

Margo looked at Leo with narrowed eyes. 'What is going on?'

'You'll see.'

They stepped out onto the first floor of the tower, saw the city stretched all around them. The platform was completely empty, as was the upscale café.

'What…?' Margo began, and Leo explained.

'I reserved it for us.'

'The whole tower?'

'The whole tower.'

'You can't do that—'

'I can,' he answered, and Margo let out an incredulous laugh.

'No wonder you've been looking so pleased with yourself.' She moved into the café, where the elegant space was strung with fairy lights, and a table for two flickered with candlelight in the centre of the restaurant. 'Oh, Leo, it's amazing.'

'I'm glad you think so.' He pulled her to him to kiss her lightly on the lips. 'Truth be told, I was afraid you might think it all a bit much.'

'No, it's wonderful. It's perfect.'

The sheer romance of it left her breathless, overwhelmed, and very near tears. They'd come through so much together, and she loved him more than ever. More than she'd ever thought possible.

'I can't believe you hired the whole of the Eiffel Tower,' she said with a shaky laugh as Leo guided her to a chair and spread a napkin in her lap.

A waiter came unobtrusively to pour wine and serve a

first course of oysters on crushed ice before quietly disappearing.

'Some might say that it is a *bit* over the top,' she teased, and Leo grinned.

'Well, I wanted to do it right this time.'

'This time?'

He took a sip of wine, his expression turning serious and making everything in Margo clench hard in anticipation.

'When I proposed again.'

'Proposed? Leo, we're already married.'

'We had a civil service, yes.'

'You want to have another marriage ceremony?'

'No, I don't want to have another ceremony. The one we had was real and binding. But I want to do it right this time—to make a proposal we can both remember.'

'You don't—'

'I know. But I want to. Because I love you that much.'

'I love you, too. So much.'

'So…' With a self-conscious smile Leo rose from his chair and then dropped to one knee. Margo let out another shaky laugh as he took her hand in his. 'Margo Marakaios—I love you more than life itself. I love the woman you are, the wife you are, the mother you are. Every part of you leaves me awash in amazement and admiration.'

'Oh, Leo—' Margo began, but he silenced her with a swift shake of his head.

'I mean it—every word. You are strong and brave and—'

'But I've been so afraid for so much of my life!'

'And you've overcome it. Overcome so much tragedy and pain. That's strength, Margo. That's courage.'

She pressed a hand to his cheek. 'You're strong too, Leo. You're my rock.'

'And yet I lived in fear too. Fear of rejection. Whether

it was by my father or brother or you. You've helped me to move past that, Margo. Helped me to realise just how important love is. Loving *you* is.'

'I'm glad,' she whispered.

He withdrew a black velvet box. 'Then will you accept my ring?'

'Yes!' She glanced down at the sapphire flanked by two diamonds. 'It's beautiful…'

'Each stone symbolises a person in our family. Annas, you and me.' He slid it onto her finger. 'So, Margo Marakaios, will you marry me?'

She laughed—a sound of pure joy. 'I already have.'

'Phew!' Leaning forward, Leo brushed her lips with his as the city twinkled and sparkled all around them. 'Thank goodness for that…'

* * * * *